Beast Be Gone
Undead Don't Die

By A L Billington

Billington
Publishing

Copyright © A L Billington 2024 all rights reserved.

First published in Great Britain in 2024 by Billington Publishing.
www.billingtonpublishing.com

The right of A L Billington to be identified as the Author of the Work has been asserted by him in accordance with the Copyright, Designs and Patents Act 1988.

All rights reserved. No part of this publication may be reproduced, stored in a retrieval system or transmitted, in any form or by any means, without the prior written permission of the publisher, nor be otherwise circulated in any form of binding or cover other than that in which it is published and without a similar condition being imposed on the subsequent purchaser.

All characters in this publication are fictitious and any resemblance to real persons, living or dead, is purely coincidental.

1 2

ISBN: 978-1-7391516-4-5

Cover Illustrations: A L Billington

1

Supreme Witch Xenixala of Xendor, Bearer of The Widowblade, Vanquisher of Dragonswell, and pin-up model for "Which Watches For Witches Weekly" turned in her bed, nestled up in the highest tower of her castle-cum-lair-cum-storehouse. Sleep was a cruel mistress who had always taken a dislike to her.

If only she had some Elixir.

Xenixala turned again and sighed. The dim light of her bedroom revealed a vast array of trinkets and trophies on the shelves, mocking her with memories and regrets. The stone walls felt as cold as her heart. She closed her eyes and tried to clear her mind.

Something tingled in the air. She shifted aside.

Feathers danced as a blade struck her pillow. The darkened figure cursed and stabbed again.

Xenixala rolled and landed on her bedroom floor with a clunk.

There were two of them. One tall and one short, both dressed in black, silhouetted against the moonlight that beamed through the open window. Broad-shouldered, probably men.

Assassins.

'Wordsworth!' she cried out.

The short assassin held Wordsworth, the spellbook, shut.

She leapt to her feet, then ducked as the tall assassin swiped, blade glinting. The figure spun and struck again. Her hand caught the knife. The pain sent her rolling back. Blood dripped down her arm.

She needed her spellbook. She needed Wordsworth. He still wriggled helplessly in the short assassin's grip.

The tall assassin lunged again. She flicked her wrist at him. A ball of fire hit his chest. He whipped off his cloak, and the flames followed it.

Xenixala cast the spell at the second figure, who clutched Wordsworth like a shield. The assassin stumbled, fire lapping at his chest.

Wordsworth fell.

He burst open, pages glowing.

'Ice to meet you,' quipped the book as he exploded in a wave of blue.

The assassins froze—in both senses of the word. They remained standing, but now resembled a pair of ice sculptures—much like the ones at fancy feasts where the Lord has more money than sense. A light mist tumbled from their glistening forms.

Xenixala breathed a sigh. 'Good job, Wordsworth. That was a close one.' She slumped onto the bed and wiped her brow. Her heart raced faster than a pegasus on heat.

'*Too* close,' said Wordsworth, his pages riffling. 'What happened to us? Have we lost our touch?'

Xenixala tutted. 'Things haven't been the same since the Elixir dried up.' Her mind wandered to its sweet tang and ensuing tingle of power. She licked her lips. 'What happened to all our protective wards and impenetrable doors? How did they get into my tower?'

Wordsworth shuffled over to the frozen adventurers and craned his book spine to look up at them. 'I believe they are... er... *were* somewhat experienced. They appear to be assassin class, after all. Very few survive the training quests. We're lucky they wore Level Five Robes of Eversneak.'

'Which made them weak to ice magic,' Xenixala smiled. 'Very clever Wordsworth.'

Wordsworth fluttered his pages with satisfaction. 'I'm not just a pretty page, you know.'

'They must have been prepared.' Xenixala scowled. 'No one has ever come that close to defeating me.'

'What about that chap Eric...?'

'I told you never to bring him up again. Anyway, that didn't count.'

'Of course not.'

Xenixala paced up and down her bedroom, deviating her route to avoid the clutter of scrolls, swords, chests and other magical trinkets.

Somebody must want her dead—someone powerful, someone with resources, someone she had crossed and had lived to tell the tale.

But who?

2

Skwee, the goblin retched for what felt like the thousandth time. Even though death was a stench he was strangely familiar with—an occupational hazard of having worked for numerous Dark Lords. In his last career as a minion, there had rarely been a moment that he hadn't witnessed some kind of blood, which, on a good day, wasn't his. However, this smell was somehow a *lot* worse. It was death, but somehow fresher, almost as if it had been repackaged into a scented candle.

Eric, Skwee's newest boss and all-round-lovely-human, had given him a peg to put over his nostrils. However, as Skwee's goblin nose accounted for about half of his face, the peg uselessly sat atop the bridge of his snout, wobbling back and forth as they stalked through the cave, providing no relief from the smell. Because Skwee had to devote so much time to balancing, he could barely watch out for zombies. It had been very kind of Eric to offer him the peg, so Skwee hadn't had the heart to tell him it was pointless. Therefore, Skwee continued his acrobatic act while desperately trying not to throw up in the zombie-infested cavern. This was especially important after Eric's stern warnings about bodily fluids attracting the undead.

'... and even snot,' said Eric as he led the way through the cave's darkness, followed by Rose, his young human apprentice. A metal contraption, which Skwee still didn't entirely trust, chugged on her back, emitting a steady flow of steam. As they walked, their torches flickered through the many stalagmites-and-or-tites, casting ever-changing shadows. The cave was silent apart from their footsteps and the ever-dripping dampness leaking through millennia of geology. The trio each wore matching overalls and white shirts, all were faded and patchy from attempts to purge the disgusting splashes that their work attracted. Emblazoned on their chests were the words:

"Beast Be Gone - Adventuring Pest Control"

They were the first company in the land of Fen-Tessai to combine Adventuring with Pest Control. After squashing the rampant outbreak of Adventurers (a story so long and winding you could have written a whole book on it, according to Eric), Beast Be Gone had gone from strength to strength (again, according to Eric). Skwee wasn't so sure that their new method of Pest Control was much different from what they'd done before, but Skwee hadn't been around for that part, so he had to take their word for it. The main difference seemed to be that this time, they had a backup crossbow if the traps and repellent didn't work.

'Why are we here again?' Skwee whispered, glancing at a particularly spooky rock feature. He shivered as a breeze passed, making his long ears stand to attention and feel even colder in the process.

'We've been through this, Skwee.' Eric sighed. 'It's your classic zombie infestation. The King wanted this cave cleaned out for a soon-to-be profitable mining operation.'

It was difficult for Skwee to notice any defining features in Eric. It was confusing enough that all humans looked alike. But Eric appeared as if the features of every other human had been blended together to make him. His wispy brown-smattered-with-grey hair, however, would be highly desirable to the average goblin, as well as the patches sprouting from his ears, arms and neck. Unfortunately, he was stocky in a way that goblins weren't. His arm was probably about as wide as Skwee's whole body.

Rose chimed in. 'So keep an eye out for clues that might lead us to the necromancer who controls them.' The peg on her freckled nose made her Western accent even more nasally, to the point that Skwee thought she sounded almost goblin, which he found oddly reassuring. She was short for a young human but made up for it by having a lot of opinions. Skwee wondered how long her dark hair would be if she ever let it down from the bun she always wore. 'Stop the necromancer and we stop all of his or her zombies.'

Skwee was still confused, but decided to stay quiet so as not to cause a fuss. He just enjoyed being included.

A cold hand gripped his shoulder. Skwee smiled. Finally, his mentor, saviour and boss had decided to give him the physical contact he so desperately craved.

Although, come to think of it, Eric and Rose were quite far in front of him.

'Eek!' he screeched, stumbling away.

A figure loomed over him, arms outstretched. Strips of flesh dripped off its body, clothes tattered and grey, its skin as pale and green as his own. The thing was the opposite of alive.

Skwee turned and ran.

He collided with Eric and, being half his height, went headfirst into his stomach. Instead of fleeing, Eric simply chuckled to himself and shook his head.

'Don't worry, Skwee,' he said, lowering his crossbow. 'Just watch.'

There was a *whoosh*, a *thunk*, a *groan* and a *thud*.

The zombie lay motionless on the ground, a crossbow bolt protruding from its head.

'Nice shot,' said Rose.

Rose pulled a lever on her backpack, producing a mechanical arm that shimmered in the torchlight. She described her backpack as "standard issue" in The West, where she was from. The arm whirred, reached toward the newly corpsed corpse, plucked the bolt from the mush—and handed it back to Eric. Eric winced, wiped the bolt with a rag, then put it in his bag with the others.

'Waste not, want not,' he said.

Rose tutted. 'Such an Eastern expression. In the West, we say: *Waste not, why not?*'

Eric ignored her. 'This is today's first lesson: always aim for a zombie's head.'

Skwee didn't understand. Surely, everything dies when you hit it on the head. He'd learned that the hard way when he got his first pet rat. 'But why... *wouldn't* you go for the head?'

Eric smiled. 'Good question. Zombies are the only time you do. Heads are small, see? Plus, any creature with a bit of sense has a thick skull or wears a helmet.' He tapped his temple with his forefinger. 'Zombies wear rags, have skulls like melons, and kindly move nice and slow. Even a child could get 'em in the head, which is quite handy because destroying the brain is the only thing that stops 'em. That and fire, but then you've got a fire to deal with.'

'That makes sense.' Skwee found himself agreeing with whatever Eric said, even when it didn't make any sense.

'That's why zombies are a breeze,' Eric continued, 'Level One Minion, maybe Two, tops. You've got nothing to worry about.'

Eric had concocted an elaborate monster rating system that Skwee was still trying to memorise, although he suspected that Eric changed the rules every time he brought it up. He once described goblins as *Level One* and had gone red as a beetroot. He'd muttered, "Well, not *all* goblins," then had avoided explaining the system ever since.

Rose sighed. 'Well, that is a relief.'

'We can't relax just yet,' said Eric, loading another bolt into his crossbow. 'They can still bite ya. Then, you'll end up dead with a strange urge to wander around. Let's press on, shall we?'

'Was... that not the only one?' Skwee stammered.

Eric laughed and patted him on the back. 'We've only just got here! One zombie isn't an infestation. This cavern could have hundreds more, maybe even thousands.'

Skwee gulped. How was Eric able to stay so calm? He must have been insane, which made sense, as Skwee had yet to meet a sane human.

Rose tightened her nose peg as she stepped over the rotting corpse. 'They smell worse than that hobgoblin nest we cleared out.'

'Someone needs to educate hobgoblins not to defecate where they eat,' said Eric, 'and about bathing. Which is strange, considering how much they use bidets.' Eric stepped over the body, too, prodding it with his crossbow and muttering, 'Oh, and always make sure they *are* dead-dead.'

They continued deeper into the damp depths of the cavern. Every few paces, Skwee was sure that the air got thicker, and the faint groans and hissing sounds grew louder

Rose squinted at her map. 'I think if the necromancer *is* here, they'll be surrounded by the strongest lurchers in the big end chamber. Right, Eric?'

'Lurchers?' Eric scoffed. 'What's a lurcher?'

'That's what we call them in the West, lurchers. On account of all the lurching.'

'That's ruddy stupid.'

Rose tutted. 'Calling them zombies is a bit stupid if you ask me. It's not like they *zombie* around, is it? Like, what does that even mean?'

'Doesn't have to mean 'nuffing. It's just a name, like goblin—oh uh, no offence, Skwee.'

Skwee didn't see anything to be offended about, although he did like his name being mentioned.

Rose continued, 'I'd never actually seen a *lurcher* in the flesh, or whatever flesh is left, but I was always told they were quite fearsome.'

'The pong certainly is,' said Eric, wafting the flies away from his face. 'But so long as we know our exit strategy and don't take on too many at once, we'll be right as rain. Have you both put on *extra* comfy shoes, like I told you?'

'*Yes*,' said Rose and Skwee in unison.

'Good,' said Eric with satisfaction. 'We may need to do some light jogging, which is famously the best way to avoid 'em.'

They arrived at a large chamber. Eric lifted his torch high, revealing the lurching forms within. They murmured and turned towards them, eyes glazed and glinting in the light. Skwee felt his knees tremble.

'Right,' said Eric, 'Pass me the rope.'

By the time the zombies came close, Eric had attached a rope to both sides of the cave wall. It reminded Skwee of the ropes put out in front of posh inns that played loud music and needed your name on a list before they would let you in. However, this rope was far less your "fancy-red-velvet" and more your "tie-up-your-donkey-hemp".

Miraculously, the wall of zombies and/or lurchers reached a total standstill once they hit the line. It held them right by the waist, blocking their path, so all they could do was shuffle their feet and stretch out their hands, desperately trying to reach the trio. Skwee was startled by the sheer variety of their rotted outfits: bakers, farmers, blacksmiths and even Men of The Holy Mole dressed in their moleskin mole costumes. There was a zombie for almost every profession, including one dressed as a giant chicken with a butcher's logo on the chest. Had they been buried in these clothes? There was no way of knowing without listening to Eric try to explain it.

'Now,' said Eric, 'Take your pointy stick, and let's have fun.' He paused. 'Just watch out for the mess.'

Skwee's pointy stick felt heavy in his hands, but it was of a reassuring length, the key sign of a premium pointed stick. He watched Eric plunge his stick into the nearest zombie's face, disintegrating it into a splatter of dark ooze. Skwee gulped and followed suit. He thrust the weapon, accidentally cutting off his target's ear. The next thrust he did with his eyes open, which hit the mark, showering him with stinking, bitter blood. He immediately regretted keeping his mouth open. The corpse fell to the floor, and another lumbered forward to replace it.

'Well done!' said Eric with a red-splattered grin as he swung his stick simultaneously through two zombies. 'And don't worry, I brought plenty of towels.'

Rose darted back and forth, jabbing her stick while the claw on her back sliced and whirled with a mind of its own. 'This is actually quite fun!' she exclaimed.

'See, I told ya they ain't no bother,' said Eric, unfazed by the zombie that had made it past the rope and held at arm's length by Eric. Its arms spun like a windmill, but Eric just laughed and kept it still. 'All their muscles have rotted away. They're weaker than kittens.'

'Why do these necromancers even bother?' said Rose. 'They know that clockwork exists, right?'

'They do,' Eric replied with a smile. 'I think they just have a death fetish.'

Soon, piles of re-deaded-dead filled the cavern floor, and the groans went silent.

Eric wiped his brow. 'Now let's check they're all definitely back to dead, and we can move on.'

They continued like this for hours, shoring up a rope and splatting zombie after zombie. Sometimes, there would be one or two lumbering alone, but most seemed to stay in packs, which made Skwee very grateful for Eric's rope trick. After a while, Skwee's fingers became coated with blisters, but not in a good way. His back screamed for a lie-down in some hay, and his joints demanded a good soak in a puddle. By this time, the trio had more red on them than not, making it look like they'd been to a vampire's ball. Eric kept grumbling about how he should have brought more towels.

After what felt like days (and without any sunlight, it may have been), the three mercifully arrived at the final section of the cave. It was a gigantic space big enough to fit at least ten goblin warrens, depending on how big the goblin family was, of course. Skwee slumped to the ground and massaged his hands.

'Right, here we are,' said Eric with a sigh. 'Nearly done. I don't reckon the necromancer will be here, though. It doesn't seem nice enough. They prefer to be at the top of plush towers.'

There was a stirring in the darkness.

Then, the sound of clinking metal and a guttural clamour.

Rapid footsteps.

A mass of bodies surged towards them, moving at what could only be described as top speed.

Rose squinted, 'Are those... lurchers? But they're running! What are they waving? Are those weapons? Can they... hold things?'

Eric scratched his head. 'I uh, oh. No? Maybe? No. Their arms are too weak.'

The creatures careered closer, now bathed in the light of their torches.

Rose spoke fast. 'And they've got helmets, and armour and...'

'By The Holy Mole,' exclaimed Eric. 'They're Ex-Adventurers!'

Skwee tugged on Eric's overalls. 'Wha... what do we do now?!'

Eric looked down at him, face white as a demi-lich. 'Time we use our comfy shoes... and run.'

3

The Great Mage Xenixala of Xendor, Bloodletter of Blendoom, Founder of Fire, and wielder of The Breadknife of Truth, continued up the path. Dust billowed with each step, falling into the abyss on either side of the sloped track. Wolves howled in the distance, their cries for attention echoing around the desolate landscape. Had she been a weak goblin-like creature, she would have shivered.

Somebody wanted her dead. What had she done to deserve that kind of hatred? Quite a lot, probably. Practically every adventure she went on led to a series of deaths, explosions and carnage. She rarely, if ever, considered what she'd left behind. But now it was time to change all that. It was time to regain her strength and make things right.

Her destination towered ahead at the peak of her climb, the only redeeming feature of the monotonous horizon. The castle's spires were pointier and blacker than a porcupine going through an awkward goth phase, and its gravity-defying turrets lunged into the air from every angle. Red glows emanated from the openings, nearly blotted out by clouds of screeching bats as they swirled, the whole scene silhouetted by the distant setting sun.

Xenixala tutted. Textbook vampire's lair.

It was such a shame that vampires all employed the same architect. They had to. Baron Von Vorbusier had a construction monopoly for about the last three thousand years—on account of being a vampire himself. His 'international' style seemed to be more about sadism than aesthetics. Every inch of a vampire's home was a dust trap. Corridors went nowhere, details were made from literal razors, and the instability of the pointy towers led to untold deaths. As it turns out, a fallen spire puncturing your entire body was one of the few ways to kill a vampire. It was almost as if Baron Von Vorbusier felt guilty about his curse and wanted to take it out on someone who wasn't him. Xenixala had heard that his house was a pleasant cottage in the countryside.

One thing she couldn't fault him for was the magical wards. Ordinarily, she could have teleported right up to the castle gates, but Baron Von Vorbusier's ego meant you had to walk up his winding path, forcing you to admire his design for as long as possible. However, he had probably spun it as a defensive measure.

'Are we nearly there yet?' moaned Wordsworth, the enchanted tome in her arms. 'I don't think you've walked this far in about a decade.'

The harsh wind whipped at Xenixala's long black hair and robes, periodically blocking out her face in a most undignified fashion. Ordinarily, she would have been head to toe in her signature charming blue, but today she had opted for a more appropriate black. She cursed and tugged the fabric hard enough so that it learned its lesson and then continued the climb. Her legs shook with each step. 'Why, in the name of the Holy Mole, would you walk when you can float?'

She stopped and wiped the sweat from her brow, hoping Wordsworth wouldn't notice. This was pointless because their souls were inextricably bound, so he felt everything she did. Most sorcerers chose a boring cat or owl as their magical familiar at wizarding school. However, she was much smarter than that. A spellbook familiar doubled her magical power, even if he was annoyingly chatty—presumably because of all the words inside him.

'So that your legs don't turn to mush whenever you havf to hywse thhem,' muffled Wordsworth as Xenixala shoved him deeper into her robes. Wordsworth didn't actually *have* a mouth, yet every part of him was a mouth. His pages flapped open in a mouthy way, accentuated by a kind of bookmark tongue. He wriggled free and flapped to the dirt. 'Very mature. Are you sure we haven't been here before? It looks oddly familiar.'

'You're thinking of Castle Helldoom. This is Castle Vanderblad.'

'Are you sure?'

'Positive.'

'Because the spires and bats and…'

'It's a different castle.'

'And the eerie glow and everything…'

'I *said* we haven't been here. It's one of the few castles I *haven't* been to. Access to this country involves a large DLC tax.'

'Which stands for "Determined Land Collection", you know.'

'Yes, I *know*.' Xenixala rolled her eyes. 'And I generally refuse to pay for their money-grabbing scheme, especially as there's barely anything here.' She gestured to the empty mountains. 'But I don't have much choice. Someone is out to get me, and I need to be able to defend myself.'

'You mean we've been… everywhere?'

'Everywhere apart from here. At least three times.'

'Blimey. Hasn't time flown by.'

Xenixala had felt the ebb of time much more acutely after the Eric incident, which haunted her nightmares. Part of her wished she had let the world burn from the "Adventurer" scourge instead of saving it like some kind of hero. Now, there was no more Elixir. She could almost taste it at the thought—the sweet, bitter tang of power and health. Elixir turned out to be why The Dark Master had created the adventuring craze in the first place. Selling potions and swords on such a scale had been a genius stroke. If she also had the mind of a banker, it would be just the sort of scheme she would have concocted.

After defeating The Dark Master, she managed to keep him alive for almost a year, reviving him over and over again in order to use his lifeblood to make more Elixir. However, as it turned out, there was a limit on how much a human soul could manage such a thing, which she discovered to be precisely ten thousand times. She'd asked the Council of Mages about it, and they said it was something that they'd known for a millennium, but didn't want to make it public knowledge. Then people would ask too many questions about *how* they knew. Eventually, The Dark Master was more dust than man and it was over.

Fortunately for Xenixala, the withdrawal symptoms of Elixir receded at the same rate as The Dark Master did, so it wasn't quite as painful as when she'd been forced to quit "frozen goose" before. All that was left was the memory chemically seared into her senses. But now her mind had never felt clearer, and she actually had to listen to her thoughts.

It was a big problem.

It didn't help that the adventuring advances had regressed by about a decade. Finding a fully stocked Adventurer's Supply was a miracle. Most caves just had bats in them (the boring kind). The only upside was that the dungeons weren't as crowded, which meant she didn't have to share with some arrogant paladin or, worse still, a bard.

The last adventuring party she'd been involved with had ended terribly. It consisted of the sickly-sweet lovers Edwardius the paladin and Felina the bard. Somehow, the pair had found themselves coating the walls of the Elixir factory after Xenixala had gone on an Elixir-fueled rampage. She would have felt more guilty if she could remember more of the details.

Without Elixir, life felt so *slow*. There was no zing, no pizazz, no *zest*.

But even worse, she felt weak. Weaker than she could ever remember being. Those assassins were inches away from killing her. She couldn't let that happen again.

Someone badly wanted her head on a spike.

She looked up at the citadel and trudged on. Hopefully, her next task would solve all that.

Xenixala had always wondered if she would make a good vampire, a question she'd asked herself ever since she was a girl. As far as she understood, there were two types of girls: those who wanted to be a vampire and those who wanted to be *with* a vampire. She never understood the other camp. It felt like a disregard for your bodily fluids and an excuse for necrophilia.

There was just something about vampires that felt *right*. Maybe it was the all-black outfits, maybe it was the aloofness, maybe it was the fact that they were all inexplicably attractive. Who was to say? It didn't matter. She knew becoming a vampire was just the excitement she would need to make her feel alive again. Even if it did mean she'd technically be dead.

Wordsworth wriggled under her arm. 'Aren't vampires a little cliché?'

Xenixala sighed. 'Everything's cliché if you think too hard about it.'

'Or, hack, rather? You know, *done to death*—if you'll excuse the pun.'

'Not excused,' Xenixala squeezed Wordsworth a little tighter. 'And no, vampires are due for a comeback. There's always a vampire fad right around the time a new fanbase of young girls comes of age. Every five to ten years or so.'

'If you say so...'

'I do say so. It also has the added benefit of eternal youth and everlasting life. My enemies won't see it coming.'

Wordsworth huffed. 'But we already don't age or die! I lost count of how old we are after we reached triple digits. Is this because you found a wrinkle the other day?'

'That wasn't a wrinkle,' said Xenixala, cautiously rubbing her face. 'It was a crease from sleeping on sheets with a low thread count. And besides, the pig's blood and Bloatfrog intestines sorted that out.' Staying good-looking was no accident; Xenixala had a long and specific beauty regime that she had perfected over decades. The primary components were enhancements, but she occasionally threw in some kind of fresh blood or sacrifice for good measure. She was immensely happy she didn't have to slap on makeup like the common tarts at court. Her smouldering eye shadow remained perfect, whatever debauchery or mess she'd made the night before.

'Sorted for now...' Wordsworth tailed off for effect, but the effect was her clamping him shut.

'Our magical prowess combined with a vampire's strength and speed...' She trailed off with a sigh. 'Why didn't I think of it before? We'll have limitless power. Limitless. *And* everyone will be asleep while I'm awake. Any more assassins will have to rethink their sneaking. You can't sneak in during the day. Everyone knows that.'

They arrived at the castle door. Every bit of it was tangled with ornate obsidian that promised to leave scars. Since there didn't appear to be a knocker, she cast a knock spell instead, and the door rumbled.

After much lingering, the great thing creaked open and a figure emerged from the darkness. He was more of a lump than a man and garbed head to toe in black rags. He looked her up and down with his one big eye and spoke raspingly. 'We are not interested in double glazing,' he croaked, 'Or converting to The New Church of The Holy Mole, or donating to any cat fund. Good day.' He started heaving the door closed.

Xenixala flicked her wrist, and a block charm wedged it open.

The man grunted and cursed. 'I said, *good day*.'

'I'm here to see Countess Von Vanderblad,' said Xenixala. 'I sent a bird ahead, so she should be expecting me.' The bird had never returned, likely gorged on by bats. But that wasn't going to deter her.

'We've no visitors scheduled for the next three hundred years,' said the man. 'Get lost.'

'I thought you might say that,' said Xenixala with a smile, promptly turning him into a toad.

4

Eric, Rose and Skwee burst through the Beast Be Gone Shop doors. All breathed a sigh of relief as the familiar aroma of dust and oak wafted over them, momentarily relieving Eric of his pain. The shop was almost back to its former glory, with fine-panelled walls and shelves packed with books on magical creatures, guides on making repellents and jars of various pickled insects that had made the fatal mistake of getting caught. Eric winced and sat down at his desk, ignoring the trail of blood he'd left behind. If there was one thing being in Pest Control had taught him, it was how to clean bodily fluid stains.

Skwee went to his corner nest and curled up in the hay. He then gently rocked back and forth with a glazed look in his eyes. The poor creature, thought Eric. Skwee could never get a break in life. No matter what Eric got him to do, Skwee somehow found himself in the direst of peril. Only last week, Eric had asked him to hold a torch, but Skwee had nearly set fire to an entire hippogriff nest—a crime that would have cursed their next thousand generations.

Eric felt responsible for Skwee after the whole incident with The Dark Master. Skwee had been working for the overlord doing all manner of menial and dangerous jobs. Eric had rescued Skwee and given him safety. In return, Skwee had helped them stop The Dark Master's plan to dominate the world's economy with an endless cycle of adventurers addicted to his Elixir. They'd snuck into his Doom Bank and defeated him along with his undead dragon. After that, Skwee felt like family—or furniture, which was kind of the same thing.

Rose slipped, looked down at the red floor and gasped. 'You're hurt!' Her backpack emitted a sympathetic wheeze of steam as she ran over. 'What happened?'

Eric had still not become used to Rose's contraptions. Just the sound of its hiss made his brow furrow. It was as if Western gadgets tried to be as pretentious and convoluted as possible. She claimed it was technology, but he knew it was just magic with extra steps. Magical items and incantations could produce the exact same effect, only with fewer pipes and smoke, which meant they could only be doing it for attention. He categorically did not trust the claw that often appeared from her backpack. It moved with a mind of its own, and he was sure it was out for his blood. Sometimes, when Rose wasn't looking, it gave him a little nip, almost as if it were telling him to "watch it".

Eric took a bottle of Fire Whisky from his drawer and took a swig. He winced and reminded himself to buy something not so cheap next time. 'I'll be okay for now,' he said.

Rose crouched beside him and scrunched up her nose, which made her seem even more mousy. 'That looks pretty bad. We should get a priest of The Holy Mole and some healing salve…'

Eric chuckled. 'It's a bit too late for that.' He held up his leg, clenching his teeth as the wound oozed over his trousers. 'You see those teeth marks? I've been bit.'

Rose inhaled sharply. 'You don't mean…?'

'Yup. I'll be a zombie soon. Classic zombie bite.'

'Are you sure?' She was visibly shaking. 'But… but when did it happen?'

Eric thought back to their narrow escape. The screams, the sweat, the running. So much running. He'd never moved so fast in all his life. Why was running so hard? People seemed to do it all the time, and the mad ones even did it for fun. Those zombies somehow moved faster than humans, despite the contradictory fact that their bodies were a smelly mush.

'One caught me while we climbed that ladder,' he said. 'Not much I could do.' Eric thought it polite not to mention that he had been the last to climb up. It was a gentlemanly manoeuvre and one that he had immediately regretted.

Skwee snapped out of his trance, probably a reflex to the smell of blood. 'Oh, Eric!' he squeaked. 'You'll b..b..b..become a z..z..zombie!?'

'Maybe. But not if we can stop it.'

'Sooo…' said Skwee with a strange glint in his eye. 'We're going to chop off your leg?'

Eric laughed. 'No, no, that won't do it. You know how blood works, right?'

'Not really,' Skwee scratched his chin. 'How do we know it won't just turn your leg? You could have, you know, like a zombie leg? That won't be so bad.'

Eric didn't know how to tell him how stupid he sounded without being hurtful, so he just ignored the question. 'This is a transmitted curse. That's pretty deep magic. All I can do is apply Un-Undead Balm to slow the turn. After that, we'll have to find and stop the necromancer who created this specific zombie curse in the first place.'

Rose put a hand on his shoulder. 'I'm impressed you even told us. In The West it's normal is to hide a zombie bite for as long as possible. Even when your mother asks you, you deny it.'

'Yes, same here,' said Eric. 'It's because zombie curses love betrayal and irony. Necromancers have a weird sense of humour; it really gets them off. Probably because they don't spend any time with the living.'

'So how long do you think we have?' asked Rose.

'Quite a while. You eventually become a zombie at the most dramatic and ironic time possible. Like as soon as you're locked up in a room with your friends. So that's something else we need to avoid, nothing dramatic or ironic, got it?'

Rose and Skwee both nodded in unison.

'No dramatic irony,' said Rose.

'No draconic iron-ly,' said Skwee.

'And no betrayal, either,' said Eric. 'But that goes without saying.'

Rose started pacing up and down the office. 'So we have to find this necromancer, the one who created these lurchers to be different. Do you have any idea why anyone might want them to be like that?'

'Beat's me,' said Eric. 'I've never seen that kind of zombie. Like... adventurer zombies.'

Rose stopped pacing. 'How do you know they're adventurers? They could have been any old corpses.'

'They're not just any old corpses,' said Eric. 'Any old corpses don't attack in formations. Only adventurers fight one by one in turn order and clump together in groups with perfectly balanced class roles. Corpses don't wear armour or carry big weapons, either. Heck, I saw a few trying to cast spells!' Eric took a big swig of his whisky. 'But adventurers can't be zombies. It's not possible.'

Skwee wrinkled his nose. 'You're saying it's impossible and... and then you're saying it's true... but you're saying... I... what are you saying?'

Eric sighed. 'Adventurers can't be zombies. They get resurrected, which messes up the curse. Their body and soul get reset too often.'

'Unless someone found a way to get around that,' said Rose. The metallic claw attached to her backpack produced a quill, which she took and started writing on her notepad.

Skwee squealed, leaping back from the chest in the corner.

'Oh, sorry, Skwee,' said the chest. 'Didn't mean to frighten you.'

'That's okay, Larry,' said Skwee, hand on his heart, eyes bulging further than usual.

Larry the mimic clumped forward, currently in the form of a treasure chest. He'd told Eric that this was his favourite shape, which Larry thought was rather original. However, every mimic Eric had ever met had said the exact same thing, even though they could theoretically appear to be anything they wanted. Mimics were odd creatures, but he'd got to know much more about them after befriending one and letting it stay in his house. The smell was the worst part, although Larry did make for excellent security. Eric forgot he was there half the time and enjoyed the random selection of chests he would change into. It meant he could avoid updating his interiors quite so much. It was one less thing to think about.

Larry stretched and yawned, pushing the corners of his chest shape so that they poked out, and the lid—which resembled a giant mouth—lazily swung open. 'That was a jolly good nap,' he said. 'What did I miss?'

'Eric's gonna turn into a zombie,' said Skwee cheerily. 'And he'll get to experience the minion life.'

Eric couldn't think of anything worse than being a minion. It wasn't just the lack of autonomy, but rather the sheer mundanity of sitting around in the same cave twenty-four hours a day, seven days a week. It would make him wish an adventurer would come and set him on fire. Maybe that was why some minions were so easy to defeat.

'Oh, what fun!' said Larry, 'I've never tried to look like one of those.'

Eric rubbed his temples. 'Larry, remember how I told you humans *can't* change shape? I'll be stuck like a zombie forever. Or at least for as long as it takes for my flesh to rot off.'

Rose looked closer at him. 'You look awfully pale, Eric... are you sure you're alright?'

Eric coughed involuntarily into his hand. 'I'm fine, I just... need to lie down for a bit.'

Rose grabbed the whisky bottle, which was already halfway to his lips. 'And you need some water,' she said.

Skwee chimed in, 'I'll get you water, Master!' He beamed up at them. 'I'm at your service.'

'That would be very kind, Skwee,' said Eric. 'Thank you. But you don't have to call me Master.'

'Right you are, Master!' he replied with a wink, then hurried out the door, glass in hand.

Rose turned to Eric. 'The King sent us to that cave in the first place, right?'

Eric nodded. 'True... So maybe he'll know where we can look next?'

'Exactly! After we clean up, we can pay His Royal Highness a visit. He does owe us one, after all.'

The thought of getting dressed up for the palace filled Eric with dread. At least the carpets were already red if he were to leak all over them.

'So let's find this necromancer,' said Rose with a wry smile '... before it's too late...'

'What did I tell you about drama?'

'Oh right, sorry.'

5

Skwee beamed as he trotted to the well at the end of the street. The city of Porkhaven heaved with life, reminding Skwee of the time when Eric described every city surface as "teeming". Rats and other more dangerous vermin scuttled by, presumably on their way to work. Skwee had to duck and weave between the throng of civilians, none of whom glanced down at him. With each stride, more mud squelched between Skwee's toes, making him feel warm and fuzzy. He breathed in deeply, taking in the fresh-yet-stale aroma. His oversized goblin nose was perfectly attuned to the smells that other creatures considered repulsive. In great metal pans, the market vendor's month-old fish sizzled, right beside alchemists brewing volatile potions, all in front of ancient walls coated in a mysterious grey sludge. Humans, elves, dwarfs, goblins, pixies, and all flavours of magical creatures sweated and urinated in Porkhaven, so that the city dripped with their scent.

It was bliss.

Skwee arrived at the well and stood in the short queue of shabby, hunched humans. People who gathered at the city watering holes rarely looked happy or healthy. In fact, quite the opposite, which made Skwee wonder if there was some correlation. Perhaps they got sick from the added strain of trekking down to the well so often? That would be because they didn't have a fantastic and obedient servant like Skwee to help them out.

His Master needed him. A glass of water would fully rejuvenate Eric and save him from becoming a zombie. Then they can all go back to setting traps and sipping tea. No more running away from horrible, fast groaners-cum-zombies-cum-lurchers. He'd been taught to call zombies "groaners" because of all the groaning, but he knew Eric wouldn't like that, so he'd kept his mouth shut.

Eric so rarely drank water that Skwee knew he was in real trouble. Most things that touched Eric's lips came in bottles and made him wince, although whatever came in said bottles seemed to put him in good spirits, so it couldn't be that bad for him.

Skwee had never heard of water being a zombie-preventing cure before. Eric was so knowledgeable about these things that it was best not to question whatever odd theories he had. But water literally fell from the sky. So you would have thought there wouldn't be many zombies that survived the rain, yet they'd seen hundreds? It would take one good downpour and they'd be right as... rain. Skwee supposed they had been in a cave, so they could hide in shelter.

Skwee got to the front of the queue and winched up the bucket. The crank squeaked in complaint with each twist, while Skwee's joints squeaked back in return. When the bucket reached the top, he dipped in Eric's favourite glass, filling it with the murky substance. Smiling, he turned back toward the shop.

A figure loomed over him, blocking out the light.

Skwee staggered back, trying not to spill any of his precious cargo.

'Hello there, *little one*,' said the figure. 'Now, what's a thing like you doing in a place like *this*?' He was tall and burly, his face more horns than face. He wore a top hat, and a thin moustache sat where his nose ought to have been had he not been an orc. Orcs were native cousins to goblins, but at some point in their history, they must have decided that fight, rather than flight, would provide the best chance of survival. Skwee knew that flight was far superior because there were more goblins than orcs, despite the fact that goblins were some of the most actively murdered animals on the continent. That was why orcs were even taller than humans, with muscles that only illegal potions could create for humankind. Conversely, goblins thought big muscles were rather showy, whereas a nice, lithe, bony frame would make your mother proud.

'Oh, sorry. Excuse me,' said Skwee, leaping aside. 'I'm on an important mission for my Master.'

The street clamour drowned out the orc's response. Skwee smiled politely and tried to keep walking, but a hand held him by the shoulder.

'Where are you running off to?' said the orc. He crouched beside Skwee, leaning on his cane. 'I was only saying hello.'

Skwee's eyes darted around, and his heart raced. The other people of Porkhaven would never intervene to help. There was a code Eric often talked about, which he liked to call "Minding Ya Own Damned Businesses".

Skwee gulped. 'Oh yes, hello to you too. Lovely day, isn't it?'

Skwee had been instructed to talk about the weather when faced with a stranger. Eric had been very cross with him when he had asked a shopkeeper what his fingers smelled of.

The orc smiled, revealing so many teeth that Skwee wondered if he had room for a tongue. 'It is! You say you are helping your Master? That is *jolly* nice of you. I suppose he is very good to you, your Master?'

Skwee thought about this for a moment. Although he knew that other humans still treated him the same way they would a mule or cat, this was still ten times better than any of his previous Masters. With them, you'd have been lucky to wake up with all of your body parts still attached.

'Yes, very well indeed,' said Skwee. 'My Master lets me sleep in lovely warm hay, teaches me all about his business, and I get as many leftover scraps as I can eat.'

'Only scraps?' The orc twiddled his moustache. 'Oh dear. A good Master doesn't just give out *scraps*. My Master gives his minions a *feast*. Twice a day!'

'Twice a day...?' Skwee's mind wandered to the one time Eric had left him a whole pigeon pie rather than just the crust. It had been heavenly—at least twice as good as eating a raw pigeon that you'd caught yourself.

'Yes!' exclaimed the orc. 'My Master also has a *fabulous* healthcare plan. *Fabulous*. Does your Master provide a healthcare plan?'

Skwee wasn't entirely sure Eric ever had any plans. What he did know, however, was that health was not especially valued in Beast Be Gone. Skwee had nearly been eaten at least a dozen times, most recently after an unfortunate incident with some hippogryphs who'd got disgruntled after someone nearly set their nest on fire.

'I don't think so, no,' said Skwee. 'But I give my Master back rubs sometimes, which he says is good for his health.'

The orc tutted. 'Good for *his* health, maybe, but what about *your* health? You're a scrawny young goblin, you need to be taken care of.'

Skwee beamed at the compliment. 'That would be quite nice, I suppose.'

The orc extended a hand. 'The name's Catcher, by the way. But my *friends* call me Catch.'

Skwee took his hand, and his whole body wobbled as they shook. 'Nice to meet you, Catcher. I'm Skwee.'

'*Catch*, please.'

'Right.'

'Listen, Skwee,' said Catcher with a grin. 'It sounds like your Master still has much to learn about properly caring for a goblin of your *calibre*.'

'You have made it sound like that, yes.'

'So how about this: Why don't you come with me, and I'll show you how *my* Master does things? Then you can return to your old Master and show him how it's done. You'll be back before he even knows you're gone.'

The centre of Skwee's head felt a slight twinge, almost as if an alarm were going off inside his skull. Wasn't there something he was supposed to be doing?

If it were that important, he would have remembered it.

'That sounds like a great idea,' said Skwee. Eric would be so proud of him for trying to improve Beast Be Gone and making new friends. 'I suppose a little look couldn't hurt. My Master is always saying how I should "think-for-myself".'

'Marvellous!' exclaimed Catcher. 'Then let us make haste. There is no time to waste! Just step into my wagon here, and I'll have you back quick-as-a-flash.' He pointed his cane down a side alley to a cart with skulls blotted onto its white canvas top.

In Porkhaven, dark alleys were supposed to be avoided at all costs, but standing next to a burly orc practically guaranteed being left alone. Therefore, Skwee saw no issue in being led into one by Catcher, his new friend.

Skwee clambered into the back of the wagon without spilling a single drop of water. He was very pleased with this, but it was too late by the time he realised why, as the horses whinnied and the cart lurched into motion.

Eric would have to wait a little bit longer.

Hopefully, it may rain soon, anyway.

6

High Seer Xenixala of Xendor, Hero of Evermoor, Legend to The Riverfolk and Speaker at the Symposium of Sycophancy squinted as she entered the main chamber of Castle Vanderblad. It was impossible to make anything out. There wasn't a single inch inside the castle that wasn't black.

Wordsworth quivered under her arm. 'Are you *sure* about this, Xeni...? I've got a bad feeling...'

Xenixala ignored him and muttered, *'Nightius visionious.'* The room appeared before her as if by magic, because it was. She could have probably waited for her eyes to adjust, but what was the point of magic if not for making your life more convenient? Looking up, it felt like she was in one of the ancient Churches of The Holy Mole. The ceiling stretched so high that clouds had formed, partially concealing thousands of buttresses and gargoyles that stared at her as if to say: "can someone get us down from here?" A black carpet led to the end of the chamber, where a droop (or whatever the collective noun was) of vampires sat around. Some leaned against the stone columns, while others lay on the floor, blowing bubbles with what appeared to be red bubblegum. A few glanced at her, rolled their eyes and returned to doing nothing.

Xenixala saw this as her opportunity to introduce herself. She cleared her throat and marched towards them.

'I am High Seer Xenixala of Xendor,' she spoke in a husky tone. All the books on vampire relations emphasised that a husky voice was the only one they took seriously. 'Hero of Evermoor, Legend to The Riverfo-'

'Yes, yes,' the tallest and best-looking vampire cut her off with a wave. She stood up from her bat-shaped chair. 'We know who you are.' A thin, blood-red crown held her luscious white hair perfectly still. 'Xenixala of Xendor, your *reputation* precedes you.'

'That will save me some time then,' said Xenixala, stopping a healthy distance away. 'I presume you got my letter, Lady Vanderblad?'

Lady Vanderblad tutted. 'I don't *read* letters. That's why we have servants. Where is Eyegore, anyway? He's supposed to turn riffraff like you away.'

Xenixala prickled. 'He *hopped* away from his duties.'

'I see. Ah, well, there's plenty more where he came from. Village folk practically grow on trees.' She looked Xenixala up and down. 'So what is it you so *desperately* want? You're not one of those silly vampire hunters, are you? The DLC was supposed to be a turn-off to adventurers and the like. They do loathe paying the levy...'

Xenixala smiled. The Determined Land Collection tax had only put her off for so long. 'If I were, you would already be dead.'

Lady Vanderblad let out a hearty laugh that echoed in the empty hall and revealed her white, pointed fangs. 'I like your confidence. False though it is.'

Xenixala cast her gaze to the vampires slothing in the corner. 'You don't seem to be the most *lively* bunch. I thought I saw a moth push one of them over.'

Lady Vanderblad waved her hand. 'They're just hungry. It is nearly lunchtime, after all. In fact, would you mind if we fed?'

'So long as you don't expect me to be dessert, it's fine by me.'

'Excellent.' Lady Vanderblad clapped her hands, and a side door creaked open so loudly it could have had a "spooky charm" on it.

Two men appeared, both of whom looked identical to the doorman. They hobbled in, dragging a great cage on wheels. Inside were two young men wearing oversized leather armour and brandishing swords that—if Xenixala were not mistaken—were the cheapest kind that Adventurer's Supply had to offer. Often marketed as "*Level One Rusty Blad*e".

'Wait until my father hears of this!' one of the men yelped. He swung his sword into the darkness, not knowing which way to look.

The other sat crouched, rocking back and forth, whimpering. 'Shut up, Errol, this is all your fault. We're gonna be vampire chowder.'

'It's not my fault! This DLC area was supposed to have so much potential!'

'I told you about all the bad reviews! You should have known!'

'People are just salty about having to pay,' Errol tutted. 'It's still quality adventuring.'

Lady Vanderblad licked her lips. 'Very fresh indeed.' She turned to the other vampires. 'Come, my brethren, it is time to *feast*!'

What happened next could only be described as a blood bath, because bathing and blood were the primary components. Xenixala didn't flinch. Her eyes had long become bored at the sight of blood, yet the tang in the air still made her heart flutter. Who was she to deny it? There was something so exciting about the look of death in someone's eyes right before you poked them with something sharp. And that feeling always went hand in hand with the unmistakable whiff of fresh blood. Feelings of shame and guilt immediately followed it. However, those feelings could be pushed deep down and forgotten about.

She was just glad she brought black robes.

The droop of vampires finished their frenzy and fell away, panting. The two servants reappeared carrying buckets and mops, then silently began cleaning with a promptness that suggested they shouldn't be the ones to be mopped up next.

Xenixala frowned at the glistening red Lady Vanderblad. 'I thought you vampires were all about the thrill of the hunt. Where was the fun in that display? It was like shooting arrows at a goblin in a barrel.'

Lady Vanderblad wiped her face, then licked her fingers in an unnecessarily seductive fashion. 'When you have hunted for the millionth time over the last ten thousand years, it becomes a little... dull. What would be the human comparison?' She tapped her chin and became distracted again by the blood on her fingers. 'Would you ever require a sand...*wedge* instead of a lavish banquet?'

Xenixala thought of the herring and onion sandwiches available on the streets of Porkhaven and shuddered. 'I *suppose* so. But hunting is your whole thing. *I'll* never tire of the hunt once I'm a vampire.'

'Ah.' A grin crept onto Lady Vanderblad's face. 'I should have guessed. You wish to become one of us.' She folded her arms. 'And what makes you think I should allow it?'

'Let me put it this way. Either you turn me, or this place burns to the ground. Your call.'

Lady Vanderblad's expression never faulted. 'I see. You are aware that becoming a vampire means losing your soul...'

'Priests invented souls to scare children. I'll be fine.'

Lady Vanderblad smirked and looked down at Wordsworth in Xenixala's arms. Wordsworth wriggled deeper into the folds of fabric.

'You have a deal, *Xenixala of Xendor,*' she said. 'I shall grant you your wish.'

'Excellent,' said Xenixala with a satisfied smile. 'In which case, I have some questions...'

'Oh.'

Xenixala produced a scroll from her sleeve and let it unfurl. It rattled down to the cobbles of the floor. 'Question one: What's with all the black and red? What have you guys got against colour?'

Lady Vanderblad hesitated. 'You'll see.'

'A vague, mysterious and ominous answer. That's on-brand, I suppose.'

'Indeed.'

Xenixala moved her finger down the scroll. 'Question two: I hear that vampires sparkle in the sunlight. But as you can't go into the daylight without turning into a flaming lump of coal, how could anyone know?'

'I think you answered your own question.'

'Nobody knows or cares. Got it. Question three: is it true that all vampires can turn into bats?'

'It is.'

'Excellent. Follow-up question: what is it like to see by using echolocation?'

'It defies explanation.'

'Urgh, fine. I'll just have to find out for myself. How about this: as a bat, do you find other bats attractive, and if so, do you ever, *you know*.' She winked.

Lady Vanderblad scratched the back of her neck. 'Only if the other creature is, too, a vampire bat.'

'I see. Does that count as bestiality?'

Lady Vanderblad stared at her coldly.

Xenixala unfurled more of the scroll. 'Too personal? Sure, next question, do you identify as undead?'

'A part of us is dead, therefore, yes. Many would consider us undead.'

Xenixala nodded. Once turned, she'd get lumped in with zombies, skeletons, ghosts and lichs. Not your usual crowd, but most people avoid them like the plague (often because they spread it). It would also mean that paladins, such as her ex-party member and now-dead Edwardius, would be terrified of her. They had a real bee in their bonnet for things that "should have stayed dead". For some reason, they made it their whole personality. 'I can cope with that. Next, do you need a coffin to sleep in, or is that just because it looks cool?'

'We sleep in coffins because it is the last place adventurers come to look.'

'That doesn't make any sense. If you always sleep in coffins, that's the first place I would look.'

'I've lived for thousands of years, and they have not found me during my slumber. Of course, it works.'

'If you slept in a *clown* outfit, you'd also be alive today. I wouldn't attribute luck to success.'

Lady Vanderblad frowned. 'Why would I sleep in a clown outfit?'

'It's just an... never mind.' Xenixala sighed. 'OK, do your fangs ever cut your own mouth?'

'Incessantly.'

'Checks out. Can you drink your own blood? You know, as a snack?'

'Would *you* ever eat your own flesh as a snack?'

'Of course not.'

'There you are then.'

'I see. Next question. Do you have to bite someone's neck to turn them into a vampire, or is that just because it's a bit kinky?'

'The neck is where the major arteries flow. And it's at the perfect height for the feast.'

Xenixala didn't doubt that both the vampire and the victim secretly enjoyed the necking part. 'How about this, do vampires need to go to the privy? And if so, does said excreta come out red or...?'

'Enough!' screamed Lady Vanderblad. The air thundered with her words. 'I tire of these inane questions. It's time for you to get what you deserve.'

'Someone needs to take a Chill Potion...'

Vanderblad lunged, teeth bared, eyes red with bloodlust.

Xenixala had a split second to tilt her neck in Vanderblad's direction.

The pain was unlike anything she'd ever felt. It burned in a way that bore into her very being, but simultaneously, it was kind of sucky.

She quite enjoyed it.

7

Standing in the throne room doorway, Eric readjusted his belt for the thousandth time that morning as if doing so would somehow make his gut magically smaller. Some exotic belts had charms for such things, but that was wishful thinking. It was the belt he had owned all his life, and if it did actually have any magical enchantments, he would have known about them by now. He also only owned three pairs of breeches and the particular pair he'd put on that day he reserved for special occasions. Because of this, he hadn't put them on for about a year, and he was still grappling with the implication of how tight they were. Perhaps a mouse had been slowly stealing bits of fabric in the night and sewing them back together?

He sighed. Who was he kidding? His body was soft in all the parts it shouldn't be. The next time he was at Mrs. Miggins "Pies and Dies" pie shop, he would have to ask her if her famous 'Mystery Pie' might contain extra mystery calories. Finally having money had become somewhat of a health hazard.

Rose looked up at him. 'Are you nervous?' she asked with a reassuring smile. 'You look nervous.'

Eric preened the sides of his wispy hair, ruining the hour he'd spent combing out as much of the grey as he could. 'A little bit, how about you?' It hadn't helped that to get into the palace, they had to walk along the avenue of heads-on-spikes of anyone silly enough to break the ever-changing rules laid out by the mostly-sane King.

Rose beamed. 'Not at all, I'm rather excited.' Her golden backpack gave a slight wheeze in agreement. She had polished both their boots the night before, and they gleefully glinted black against the red of the carpet.

'Lucky you.'

Eric took a deep breath and stepped into the throne room, trying not to limp as the throb of the zombie bite shot through his body with every step. His foot had now turned the purple shade reserved for royalty and oozed in a way that only dead things do.

The King leapt from his throne as soon as he spotted the pair. 'Eric and Rose! What a pleasure to see you both!' The King had a presence that screamed privilege. Not just because his luscious cloak could have paid off the entire city's student loans, but the way he spoke and moved somehow implied that everything was his and that the hardships of life were someone else's problems. 'Where's the other one? The little man with the funny nose?'

Eric bowed, bringing him to eye level with The King. 'Skwee?'

'That's the fellow! Skween.' The King's grey whiskers wobbled as he spoke, indicating that he did indeed have a mouth hidden under there somewhere.

'Right. I left him to manage the shop. Although I haven't seen him today.'

'Excellent idea, always a good idea to delegate things to the lowly sorts. Now, how can I help you? Did you manage to sort out that zombie mess? The cobalt mining operation there will be *most* lucrative.'

'Yes, well about that…'

Rose stepped forward. 'There was an incident, sire. The Lur… *zombies* were faster than normal. They seemed like they were… adventurers.'

The King drew breath, and the oversized crown slid over his eyes. He pushed it back up with a finger. 'Adventurer zombies? Impossible. You must be mistaken.'

'Afraid not, sire,' said Eric. 'They're like nothing we've ever seen. We were lucky to get out alive.' Eric shuffled the weight onto his good leg.

'Oh my.' The King slumped back into his throne. 'And I was thinking we had adventurers under control at last.'

Eric nodded. 'You can't exactly ask a zombie for his adventuring permit.'

The King smiled knowingly. 'You wouldn't believe how much we've made selling those permits. Just about paid for all the damage those adventurers did to the city.'

'That was at least half the bandits' doing.' Eric scratched the back of his neck at the memory of The Bandit King's head rolling at his feet. Sometimes, he'd dream about it and wake up in a cold sweat. Eric had given the bandits the idea to fight back against the adventurers, but they'd got a little more 'looty' than he'd expected. The whole city of Porkhaven had become a war zone. Since then, Eric had noticed people gave him a much wider berth when he walked down the street.

'Well, that's why I introduced the Theft Permit too. No unauthorised thieving or looting ever again! The chaps I put in charge of that have started calling themselves *The Thieves Guild*.' The King tutted and shook his head. 'Sounds a little *grand*, don't you think?'

'I suppose so.' The idea of authorised theft sounded nonsensical. 'But most bandits ended up in your army, didn't they?'

'Of course! And a fine job they're doing, too, rounding up any loose, unlicensed adventurers, not to mention any unruly minions coalescing into rag-tag armies of their own. The whole thing has been a logistical nightmare.'

Eric decided not to mention that The King's vizier-slash-accountant had caused the whole adventuring mess in the first place.

The King had definitively profited from the evil scheme. But Eric held his tongue as he valued his head as an attachment to his body rather than an adornment to something pointy. 'And do you have a new vizier now?'

'I shall be interviewing people for the job very soon!' The King waved his hand as if it were no longer an issue. 'Although I have decided to rebrand the role for the *optics*. The role shall henceforth be known as *The Fist of the King.*'

'Oh. Isn't that a little... you know?'

'A little what, my boy? A fist is the strongest part of the body, and it hangs at my side, ready to strike! I'm always ready for a jolly good fisting. It's the perfect title.'

'Indeed it is, sire.'

'The Porkhaven sewers have been in total shambles of late. Sorting out all the bunged-up refuse pipes is the perfect job for The Fist. Anyway, we digress.' The King stood up and began pacing back and forth. 'What is to be done about these not-dead-but-dead adventurers running amok?'

Eric cleared his throat. 'We were hoping you might know something. Have any of your spymasters heard anything?'

'Quite a few of them have gone missing lately.' The King sighed. 'Spies are tricky to keep track of at the best of times. Very good at hiding, you see.'

'I can imagine.'

'And you're *sure* there wasn't a necromancer hiding in that cave?'

'Not that we could see,' said Eric. 'But someone has to have created the curse, and they can't be too far away, or the magic would wear off.'

The King stroked his whiskers and looked up at the ornate panelling on the ceiling. 'Thinking about it, I did hear the name of a necromancer the other day. Some townsfolk were complaining about the smell he was making. What was his name? Simon... Steven? *Steven* Rotbarrow, I think? Steven, with a "V". Has a tower on the west side of Porkwood forest. Perhaps he's the chap to blame.'

'Well, it's a start, I suppose.' Why was it that necromancers always lived in towers? It must have been an ego thing. Or something to do with repressed urges with body parts resembling towers.

Rose did a little jump with joy. 'A lead! How exciting!'

Eric's heart sank. He'd rather lie down with a whisky and his leg eased up on soft pillows. It would have been much simpler if The King sorted his own problems for once. If ever any fort and cave had a hint of unwanted residents, then Beast Be Gone was summoned. At least the money was good.

'Marvellous,' said The King. 'Oh, and by the way. If you don't find this necromancer, I'll be sure that you become part of his army.' The King gave a hearty laugh that suggested he was joking. Eric swallowed hard. He knew that he wasn't.

Although, the point was moot, considering the bite on his leg. The thought of which he found oddly reassuring.

8

Skwee hurried along the corridor, being careful not to spill the glass of water. The glass in question hadn't left his hand since Eric had given it to him. He'd only spilt three drops in as many days, and his arm ached worse than when he was chief palm leaf wafter for a surprisingly sweaty master. The corridor was much like any other evil overlord's lair. There were passages going nowhere, barricades, dark wall hangings, nondescript torches, and hidden rooms that held just one specific piece of treasure. It even *smelled* like his old master's lair—a mix of fresh goblin sweat and dust.

He continued his search and took a left turn down another tunnel. Skwee hadn't been able to find Catch since he had dropped him off here, wherever *here* was. The wagon journey had been deathly dull, and with the tarp pulled tightly, he hadn't the foggiest idea where he'd been abandoned.

Eric needed his water, and if Skwee didn't get home soon, Eric would become a horrible evil zombie. Skwee didn't know what he would do if Eric turned undead. Getting used to the smell would probably be the trickiest part, although the jobs might get a little less dangerous.

Some goblins hurried past him, yet none paid him any mind as usual. They must have *really* yearned for their master's approval, which was good news for the master and bad news for the goblins. Whoever the master was of this dark operation, they sure ran a tight ship. This was both comforting and terrifying, as the best things often were.

Skwee was tempted to ask someone for directions, but he didn't want to be a bother. Everyone seemed incredibly busy, even though Skwee wasn't entirely sure why.

He turned yet another corner, and there it was, finally, the door he'd been looking for. A sign over it read "Goblin Resources" in splattered green paint. He took a deep breath and clunked his hand onto the wood.

'Enter,' came a squeaky voice—unmistakably goblin.

Skwee entered the tiny room, which would have barely fit a human. A single goblin sat in front of an upturned crate.

'New recruit?' she demanded without looking up from her scroll.

Skwee nodded. It was better to be agreeable. People were nice to you when you agreed with them.

The goblin pushed her tiny spectacles up her nose with an extended finger. 'Name?'

Skwee hesitated. 'Skwee.'

'Past master's name?'

'Um, I've had a few, but my last master was The Dark Master. I think he's dead.'

The goblin nodded and, to Skwee's surprise, scrambled up the wall.

Skwee looked up. The ceiling stretched so far you couldn't even see the top. Along the walls sat thousands of scrolls, nestled neatly in rows. The goblin continued to climb up into the distance, leaving Skwee to stand and think about his life choices.

Two moments later, the goblin returned with a scroll between her teeth. She went to her desk and unfurled the paper, raising her eyebrows as she read.

'Skwee, you say? My my, this is quite the career you've had.'

Skwee shuffled from foot to foot. 'I suppose so.'

'It says here that you used to be The Dark Master's right-hand goblin?'

'That's true. But you see, I still have another master...'

'As well as a real estate agent...'

'And I'd quite like to go home now...'

'Tea boy...'

'Can someone take me home?'

'Shop assistant...'

'Please...?'

'And all-round high-level minion.' The goblin looked over her spectacles at Skwee. 'Is all of this true?'

'Yes.' By this, he meant that he would indeed like to go home. But as soon as he said it, he realised she'd asked about his career. Luckily, the answer to both questions was yes. However, he got the impression that she thought having a varied career like his was actually a *good* thing. When really, he had failed so miserably at each job that they'd kept moving him around, with every department wanting to pass the problem on to the next.

The goblin scribbled something onto a bit of paper and stamped it. She handed it to Skwee, her face impassive. 'Go to Level Ten, show them this and ask to speak to The New Master. He'd like to see you.'

'Speak to The New Master?' Skwee's hands started to shake. 'But... why me?'

'Lord Edwardius has requested to speak with all high-level recruits immediately.'

'Oh.'

The name Edwardius sounded familiar, but he was certain he had never met anyone called Edwardius in his life.

Maybe he was an old friend of a friend.

9

Mistress Diviner Xenixala of Xendor, Baroness of Secrets, Defeater of The Monster of Krakatoon, and constant nuisance to The River Folk who just want a quiet life, *thank-you-very-much*, realised she had never actually felt true pain before that day. Sure, she'd been sliced, stabbed, impaled, burned and flayed. But this had been worse. Much worse. Before, most of her injuries had been immediately healed by magic or Elixir. That pain was short-lived. Somehow, knowing that everything would be fine had its own healing properties.

This, however, was *real* pain.

It was so excruciating that it made her want to tear her eyes out because that would hurt less and take her mind off it.

Her blood felt like it was boiling. Her skin prickled and jabbed. Every organ was in overdrive. Every drop of her bodily fluids had long since been purged.

She lay on her bedroom floor, nestled atop the tallest tower of her impenetrable fortress. Alone (except for Wordsworth, but he didn't count), breathing as deeply as she could.

Eventually, the sun set on the worst day of her life, and the pain finally stopped. The moonlight shone through the open window, revealing the hundreds of useless and priceless trinkets adorning the walls: crowns, deeds, keys to kingdoms, golden awards, silver awards, platinum awards, magical swords, enchanted boots, gilded boxes, lost heirlooms, thank you letters, taxidermied monster heads, and dozens of books where she'd been featured in the acknowledgements. A lifetime of work.

It all paled to what she had achieved today.

She looked over at her pillow, still sliced in half. She did this to protect herself. She needed to become strong again. She just hoped it was worth it.

That filthy vampire had tricked her. Vanderblad had known the vampire's curse was immensely painful and had conspicuously decided not to mention it. Being eaten had been bad enough, but then being forced to drink the Countess' blood had been truly stomach-churning.

Xenixala had: '*How painful exactly is the transformation?*' on her list of questions but hadn't managed to get that far before being rudely interrupted. She made a mental note to exact some kind of revenge when she felt better.

No.

There should be less revenge. Revenge was what sent assassins to her bed. She needed to atone, make amends, change her image. Use her power for good. Then, no one would dare cross her again.

She sat up slowly. The room spun. She wiped her brow, her skin cold as marble, then looked down at her hands. They'd turned an ivory white, her nails black and sharp to a point. A grin crept onto her face as pain shot through her mouth. The metallic tang of blood burst across her tongue. She sent a curious finger in to investigate her teeth, but the finger regretted its decision and came out as if a razor blade had sliced it. That would take some getting used to.

She stood up and steadied herself on the full-length mirror she'd been awarded for saving a township from a spider-worshipping cult.

'Oh!' said the mirror. 'Who's... there?'

'It's your mistress, Xenixala.' She looked into the glass and saw... nothing.

It had worked.

'An invisible charm,' said the mirror. 'Very clever. But if you want me to do my job, you better switch it off.'

Xenixala smiled and felt her fangs descend. 'There's no switching *this* off.'

Time to see what else she could do. She went over to her notice board and pulled down one of the posters she'd collected the day before. Some bandits had been terrorising trade caravans. Guild offering reward to stop them... yadda yadda. The perfect quest to improve her reputation. Nobody liked bandits, not even other bandits.

How does one turn into a bat? Perhaps you had to think batty thoughts.

Flap. Flapping? Night time. Bugs.

Yummy bugs.

Upside down.

Screech?

There was a *poof* sound; instantly, she felt light like a feather. Had the room just got bigger, too? No. She was smaller. *Much* smaller. She raised her arm, but she saw a horrid skin flap. Not just skin, a wing.

Time to fly.

Thonk.

Why was there a forcefield blocking the window? Had she cast a protective spell and forgotten about it?

THONK.

That one really hurt. How was she supposed to fly dramatically into the night when she'd trapped herself inside her own house?

Thonk.

Oh, right, glass. If she had cheeks, they would have gone beetroot. With that, she flapped into the night sky through the half-open window.

The outside air felt cool, and alive with smells and sounds. It was as if she could taste the ground hundreds of feet below and feel the rustle of every leaf.

Bat vision was not something she could really articulate. When she bellowed, she saw the world anew, mapped out in three dimensions (a few dimensions less than she was used to) perfectly in her mind's eye. It was like trying to explain the colour blue to a blind person. You would just say "the sky", "you know" and "blue" a lot.

Time to test out her power.

She was high above Porkwood now. There were always plenty of bandits in Porkwood. She could hear their hearts racing far below, deep in the bushes, their juicy blood coursing through their bodies. They didn't need all that blood, it was only fair to let her borrow a bit. Or most of it.

The bandit community had taken quite a blow after Eric had got involved and ruined their whole economy. The Bandit King had sided with The Dark Master to fuel an endless cycle of theft and wholesaling adventuring loot—with little regard to the lives of the bandits themselves. After Eric killed The Bandit King and started a riot, the bandits scattered like cockroaches. This made them weak. Easy prey for her to start with.

Xenixala descended through the trees and landed in front of a fort. Moss grew up on the sides of its wooded palisade, coating the gaps where the wood had rotted away. The stench of unwashed men and fear told her it was packed with thieves.

How did you turn back into a human again? Not human. Vampire. How did she turn back into a vampire again?

Think vampire thoughts.

Blood.

Teeth.

Counting.

Hiss?

Poof. The world shrank.

Xenixala blinked, forgetting that it was nighttime. *'Nightius visionious,'* she muttered. But for some reason, the world actually got darker. She dispelled it, and everything came back into view, yet all a shade of grey. Was this vampire-vision? It was clear, but lifeless, like an overcast afternoon at the Porkhaven docks. She would have to find a way around that.

Someone tapped her on the shoulder. She spun around. How had she not smelled them creep up?

A translucent glow hovered before her. It had the vague shape of a person mixed with a bed sheet. It held a clipboard and wore an official-looking hat. 'Evening,' it said.

Xenixala glared at the spirit. 'Yes?'

The spirit cleared its throat, despite not having one, in an attempt to sound official. 'I see you're about to raid this thief's lair here.'

'Bandit lair. What of it?'

'Thief's lair.'

'What?'

'They identify as thieves now. A bandit is a slur. They have a union.'

'I don't care.'

The spirit held up a finger. 'This operation is legal and all above board.'

'If you say so. What do you want?'

'Licence and registration please.'

Xenixala hesitated. 'I don't have it on me. You *just* saw me arrive as a bat. Bats don't have pockets.'

'But you're wearing clothes with pockets.'

Xenixala hadn't really thought about it. 'Oh, right. I don't have my adventuring licence, it's at home. So leave me alone.'

'I'm afraid I can't do that. Section four-six-two-three of The King's new decree states that...'

'No adventuring without a licence, yeah, yeah, I know. Tell The King he can come after me for the fines if he dares.'

'It won't just be fines, ma'am.' The spirit produced a comically large horn from his ethereal robes. 'I will also be forced to notify the minions of this lair of your presence, giving them a chance to evacuate.'

Xenixala sighed. All these new rules for adventuring sapped the fun out of things. A solution coalesced in her mind like clotted blood. 'I'm a vampire. I don't need a licence.'

'Ah, I see. So you're a minion.'

Xenixala huffed. 'I am no minion!'

The spirit looked down at his clipboard. 'It says under section seven-six-five: Vampire, Level Thirteen minio...'

'I am *not* a minion.'

'Do you want me to book you or not?'

'Urgh, fine. Call me whatever you want. Your opinion means nothing.'

'Just doing my job, ma'am.'

Xenixala mumbled something about a troll's nether regions and strode away.

'You have a good night now,' called the spirit behind her.

There was nothing worse than a jobsworth. Especially one that she couldn't strangle. Now it was time to murder some bandits. They deserved it. After all, they were murderers themselves.

She could feel the strength of the vampire's curse already. It was not unlike the effects of Elixir. A tingling sensation of power with every movement. But this felt darker. There was a thirst for death inside of her. A lust for blood, carnage and control.

She let the feeling absorb her as she stalked into the camp, clinging to the shadows.

A dozen men sat around a pitiful campfire, roasting rats on sticks and making banal comments about the weather. The flames illuminated their bandana-covered faces.

Xenixala licked her lips, cutting her tongue on her fangs in the process.

She cursed under her breath.

'What was that?' said a bandit, turning his head.

'Hmm, must have been the wind,' said another.

Xenixala pounced.

Flesh and blood flew in all directions. Her speed was unmatched. Her claws cut like butter. Her thirst raged. Her taste buds sang with glee. She drank and drank and drank. She laughed and rolled in their death.

Nothing compared to that. Not Elixir, not even adventuring.

Nothing.

It was the best night of her life.

10

Eric and Rose arrived at the bottom of the necromancer's tower. It pierced through the surrounding trees and up into the clouds. Vines and cracks traversed the otherwise smooth, round sides.

Eric wiped his brow and dismounted Maisy, the mule. Why was it so hot this time of year? The fever must be setting in. They didn't have much time. This necromancer had better be in charge of these wretched zombies, or he was done for. Maybe he'd prefer his life as a zombie. Fewer responsibilities certainly seemed appealing. He could live like Skwee, who got to look after the shop while they ran around hunting corpses. Although come to think of it, Eric hadn't seen Skwee that morning. He may have been distracted by a turnip-shaped cloud again.

Rose slid off her steed, the oversized chuffer. She took off her goggles and looked up. 'I'm not looking forward to climbing that thing.' Her chuffer let out a wheeze of steam as hundreds of legs retracted beneath its great metal carapace. Eric liked to think of the Western contraption as a big woodlouse, which made him hate it a little less. All the steam and noise was ostentatious.

'Nor am I, but here we are.'

They prepared their gear and bags and then went to the entrance to the tower, a plain wooden door with a brick surround.

Rose put her back against the wall beside the door. 'So are we knocking, or…?'

'Don't be daft,' said Eric. 'We're doing this the adventuring way. These new zombies are too much for our traps.'

Rose produced a metal bomb from her pocket. 'Right.'

Eric steadied his shaking hands against his crossbow. 'Ready?'

'Ready.'

Eric kicked the door. It fell inward with ease, crashing against its hinges. He was immediately reminded that age is not kind to knees. He cursed as the pain shot through his non-zombie-bitten leg.

'You could have at least *tried* to use the handle,' said Rose.

Eric grunted, then entered the darkness within.

The rancid smell hit them like a slap in the nostrils. Rose retched, and Eric steadied himself on the wall. He held his breath and fumbled for the nose pegs in his pocket. He applied his first, then handed the other to Rose.

Rose spluttered and spat on the stone floor. 'The lurcher stink here is even worse than before!'

'Indeed, although I'm not sure if that's a good or a bad thing.'

Eric lit a torch and held it high, revealing an empty entranceway with columns lining the sides and a set of stone stairs at the centre.

To the left of the door, there was a letterbox with the words *'Steven Rotbarrow, Necromantic Services Inc.'* carved into it.

Rose read the letterbox. 'At least this is the right tower.'

'I gathered that from the smell.'

They crept up the staircase in perfect silence. As they climbed, the sounds of groaning grew louder and louder. Eric and Rose exchanged glances.

The top opened into a great hall. Bones and crude lanterns hung from the vaulted ceiling, illuminating the shambling sea of zombies below. Thankfully, the zombies appeared to be normal. None moved faster than the speed of a snail with a hangover. Their selection of apparel amounted to nothing but rotten rags.

Eric sighed with relief. Normal zombies were something he knew how to deal with.

'I was wondering, Eric,' whispered Rose, her brow furrowed. 'Why don't they eat each other, only the living? Can't they eat normal food?'

'How are they gonna manage that?' Eric whispered back. 'It's not like they have the wherewithal to whip up a risotto. They're mindless.'

'Then how come they know not to attack each other?'

'Excellent question,' said Eric, preparing his rope. 'They have an incredibly acute sense of smell. Why do you think I've not been bathing?'

'I thought you'd just been going through a rough patch. You know, with your leg and everything.'

Eric huffed and ignored her. 'That's how the ones with empty eye sockets can still track you.'

'But some of them don't have noses either! They've barely got a face left at all.'

'Oh, well, um. Those ones are probably just following the others.'

'Except the adventurer lurchers, of course.'

'You can say that again. Although I can't see any... yet.' Eric surveyed the mass of zombies wandering aimlessly around the room. He handed Rose the other end of the rope. 'Okay, you take the left, I'll take the right.'

Rose pulled the goggles down over eyes. *'Now let's kill some dead.'*

Eric lowered his crossbow, then hesitated and looked at her. 'Did you just come up with that?'

'With what?'

'That catchphrase. *Now let's kill some dead.*'

'Oh, I uh... I thought of it on the way here.'

'I thought so.'

'Do you like it?'

'Not bad, I suppose.'

'I was trying to be dramatic. But they're already dead, you see, so…'

'I got it.'

'Right.'

'Maybe we workshop it later.'

'Sounds good.'

Eric turned back to face the horde, which still hadn't noticed them. 'Here goes nothing.'

Rose extended the arm from her backpack, but it now had a circular saw instead of a claw. It whizzed and span, glinting in the candle light. Rose beamed at Eric. 'I made a few modifications last night. Pretty cool, huh?'

Eric didn't like to admit that it was possibly one of the coolest things he had ever seen. Partially because that meant accepting Western technology, but also because it would acknowledge that there was indeed a scale of cool. He would surely be in the negative numbers if such a scale existed. So he simply shrugged and leapt into action.

They ran around the edge of the room in separate directions, each holding an end of rope, releasing it as they went. They wrapped around the horde, then passed the other side, tightening their hold. Soon, the zombies were huddled shoulder to shoulder, encased by the line knotted around them. The dead feebly stretched their arms towards the pair, moaning aimlessly but going nowhere.

Eric took a moment to catch his breath. 'That's a bit more like it. Now for the messy part.'

Rose's buzz saw whirred. 'Leave it to me.'

Eric hid back down the stairs so he only got to hear the carnage. He was okay with this, as it meant he stayed dry.

Once the whizzing and splatter sounds finished, Eric returned to find the room more-red-than-not. Gristle and blood coated almost every inch, including a beaming Rose and a pile of headless dead.

He threw Rose a towel. 'Good job. But let's not hang around; that kind of noise could attract something with more teeth.'

'Gotcha.'

They moved to the other side of the room, where another stair led up into the darkness and another floor.

The next floor up was almost identical. A mass of zombies in a nondescript hall.

Eric and Rose nodded at each other in agreement, then got to work.

Rope, buzzsaw, carnage.

Another stair.

More zombies. Rope, buzzsaw, carnage.

Up again. Rope, buzzsaw, carnage.

More stairs. More zombies. More carnage.

Eventually, Eric lost count of the floors, though his knees hadn't. He stopped momentarily and stretched a leg on top of a pile of their victims. His lower back gave a satisfying crunch, and he felt slightly better.

Even Rose looked a little flush, although it could have just been the blood smears. 'It would have been nice if they'd put some windows in,' she said, 'Then we'd know how high up we were.'

'Dungeons and lairs never have windows,' said Eric. 'Saves on design fees.'

'I think we must be near the top by now. That's at least twenty floors we've cleared.'

'You're on the sixteenth floor, actually,' came a voice from under Eric's leg. Eric leapt back and whipped his crossbow towards the mass of bodies.

'Don't mind me,' came the voice. 'I'm not going to hurt you; you've done me a favour.'

A rotted face poked up from the mush. An ivory hand pulled at the skin, revealing a skeletal grin. 'I'm Tony Bones. Nice to meet you. Shoot me all you like. It'll only waste your ammo.'

Tony Bones, the skeleton, stood up from the pile, revealing his bony form layered with scraps of festering skin.

Eric lowered his crossbow, knowing it was true, although he kept his finger on the trigger. Skeletons were curious creatures. Essentially enchanted inanimate objects, it didn't matter how much you smashed them up, they'd slowly reassemble—even if it took them the next few years and spanned multiple continents.

'Hello, Mr Bones,' said Eric. 'What are you doing dressed as a zombie in a zombie lair?'

Tony Bones stepped into the open and wiped himself down. Scraps of skin fell to the floor. 'I was just trying to fit in. You know how hard it is for skeletons?'

'Not really, no,' said Eric.

Tony Bones tutted through his bared teeth. 'It's all zombies, zombies, zombies these days. No one cares about us, and we're the original undead! People just shoo me away if they see me. Say, I'm too *spooky* but not *scary*. I used to frighten people all the time just by shouting "boo", but now they only laugh. They don't even bother trying to fight me. It's embarrassing, is what it is.'

'And dressing as a zombie helps?'

'Sure does! Finally, I get some respect. Adventurers get jolly scared when I creep up on them like this. Only thing is, there are zombies *everywhere* now. How am I supposed to compete? People are nearly bored of them, too. I'll have to dress up as a dragon or something next, although I don't have the dexterity to make the costume.'

Eric nodded, knowing all too well the boredom of endless zombies. 'Why do you think there are suddenly so many zombies?'

Tony Bones tapped his chin with a finger. 'I guess people like Steven got carried away.'

Rose cut in excitedly. 'We're actually looking for Steven The Necromancer. Is he here?'

'That depends,' said Tony Bones. 'Steven with a "V" or a "P"?'

'Um, either?'

Tony Bones looked at them, expressionless. But only because his face was a skull. '*With a "P"* left long ago, it's *with a "V"* up there now.'

Rose looked at Eric. 'I think the King said Steven with a "V"? It's hard to hear him through the moustache.'

'It doesn't matter,' said Eric. 'Is there a necromancer upstairs or not?'

'Oh, for sure,' said Tony Bones. 'He's about as necromancer as they come. I'd be careful if I were you, though. He's a strange fellow.'

'Don't worry, I'm used to strange. How much further up?'

'Next floor', said Tony. 'You can't miss it.'

'Lovely,' said Eric with a grin, relieved there wouldn't be many more stairs. 'Come on, Rose, *let's kill some dead.*'

Rose frowned. 'I think you mean: *let's kill some alive* this time. The necromancer's not dead yet.'

Eric marched over to the stairway, crossbow at the ready. 'You know what I ruddy well mean.'

11

Skwee held his breath as he knocked on The New Master's door.

Knocking on doors never felt good. If the person had their door closed, they didn't want you to come in, so they were never pleased to see you. Although Skwee never felt anyone was ever pleased to see him. Except maybe Eric and Rose, but only if things were going well. He looked down at the glass of water in his hand and sighed.

'Enter,' boomed a gravelly voice through the wood.

Skwee did precisely that and found himself in what appeared to be a strange morgue. Corpses hung from the ceiling on long chains. Great vats lined the walls, glowing green and full to the brim with body parts. Skwee was about to cover his nose from the stench but stopped himself as it seemed impolite.

A man sat in the middle of the room on a crude throne fashioned of bones. At least the bones were human and not goblin. He glared intently at Skwee with glowing eyes.

'Ahh,' he spoke. 'You must be Skwee. I've been looking forward to meeting you.'

Skwee trembled. 'A pleasure to meet you too... umm.'

'They call me *The New Master*, Skwee. However, I go by many names. In my past life, they called me *Edwardius*. You may call me this if you wish.'

That seemed more appropriate, as Skwee already had another master, so he simply nodded.

Edwardius stood up and walked towards him. The man had an imposing height, amplified by his rusted paladin armour, which creaked as he moved. His pallid and wrinkled skin looked like a finger that had been left in the bath for too long. His white hair drooped down to his shoulders, which he periodically flicked back, making him seem more vain than you would expect, given his description.

'Do you take me for an evil overlord, Skwee?'

Skwee gulped. It must be a trick question. 'Urm. Yes?'

'You can be honest, Skwee, I won't hurt you.'

'Oh.' Skwee felt his shoulders relaxing. 'Then I don't know. Do you do evil overlord things?'

'I'm trying.' Ewardius sighed. 'But I'm not sure I'm doing a good job. That's why I need your help.'

'You need *my* help?' Skwee couldn't believe what he was hearing. No one ever asked for his help. They just demanded service.

'I do indeed.' Edwardius seemed to smile, but his half-rotted face made it look more like a grimace. 'I heard you had quite a lot of experience with The Dark Master.'

'I suppose I did, yes.'

'Then you are just the goblin I need.' He started to pace back and forth. 'I'm new to this game, you see…'

Skwee felt a monologue incoming. That was undoubtedly evil overlord behaviour, alright. Skwee sometimes wondered if monologing was a personality trait that evil overlords shared, as he had yet to meet one that didn't do it. Even Eric did it on occasion, although when he did, it was usually something about a recipe for knoll-repellent or complaining about "the youth of today". Perhaps they just wanted to be heard. That must be why they liked hiring so many underlings who had to do whatever they said.

'In my past life,' Edwardius continued, 'I tried to stop The Dark Master, your last overlord. However, someone got in our way. A *witch*, whose name I shall not speak—and not just because she chooses so many ridiculous titles, but because it pains me to think of her. She murdered me and my beloved Felina, by exploding us in The Elixir Factory, deep in The Dark Master's lair. I only survived as my head flew into one of the vats, and it regenerated me into the form you see before you.' He looked down at himself. 'I used to be so handsome, but now… I am a monster.'

Skwee felt sorry for the man. Most overlords didn't have a sad backstory like this. They'd just been born evil. Or at least that's how it seemed.

'You may ask, what do I have left to live for?' He gestured over to a tiny shadow in the corner of the room.

The figure shuffled into the light. Skin dripped from its tiny pixie frame, its pointed features warped and green. Flies buzzed around its head as it lurched.

Skwee yelped and jumped back.

'Do not be afraid, little one, this is just Felina. My beloved.' Edwardius shook his head. 'Look what has become of her. The vats were not so kind to her as they were to me.'

Felina stopped suddenly with a *clang*, the chain around her neck holding her still. She wheezed and held out her arms, mindlessly clawing at them, even though they were well out of reach.

'She is all I have left. Yet she is death itself.'

'That's… awful,' said Skwee.

'I have made it my mission to become what I once tried to destroy and use it to bring justice to those who wronged me. This is all that drives me now. Will you help me, Skwee? Will you help me become an evil overlord and exact my revenge?'

Skwee fidgeted with the rim of the glass of water. 'Umm, I would love to… but you see… I already sort of… have a master…'

'A dark one?'

'No, he's sort of grey-beige, if anything. But I really ought to get back to him. He'll be awfully worried by now.'

Edwardius' expression darkened. 'Skwee, I cannot make you help me, but I will not let *anything* get in my way. Do you understand?'

Skwee nodded as a drip of sweat made its way down his back.

'I am a fair master,' said Edwardius. 'I will return you home once you have shown me the path of an evil overlord.'

'Righto,' said Skwee. 'I suppose we should get cracking then.'

12

Ace Sorceress Xenixala of Xendor, Lady of The Nightfolk, Queen of The Daybound, Chief Negotiator for The Council of Wheat and Other Miscellaneous Sundries landed in front of the mouth of a cave.

Hiss. She thought, and her body reconfigured itself into a less flappy shape.

Being a bat still took some getting used to. The hardest part was resisting the urge to eat bugs and hang upside down somewhere safe. It wasn't as if it was a speedy method of transportation, either. She could just as easily have teleported; however, that didn't seem *vampire-ly.* And she wanted the full experience, even if that experience would last the next millennia.

This cave was the classic stomping ground for adventurers.

She licked her lips and entered the cavern, her eyes perfectly aligning with the darkness. Life had become almost utterly grey since her rebirth, the only upside being that the greyness was the same in the light as in the dark. The tunnel walls were straight, with rows of wonky wooden supports that suggested it had once been a mine.

She skulked deeper into the cave-cum-mine, following the faint sounds of footsteps within. Soon, she could taste her target's breath in the air, and feel the electricity of their pulse, even though they were hundreds of feet away.

They began to speak, and she could hear every word.

'More zombies! I bored of zombies,' came one voice, deep and simple. It must be a barbarian.

'There have been an awful lot of zombies of late, Gronk,' came a woman's voice. It was high-pitched and pompous—definitely a cleric. 'But they're not so bad.'

'The 'cos Panella have all kill undead spells,' said Gronk. 'No fun for us.'

Gronk and Panella. They were some of the adventurers she'd once had the displeasure of being in a party with. Xenixala had to push back the thought of petty revenge, despite it being the best kind of revenge. She was here to make amends. If people were going to hunt her down, every person she apologised to would be one less person who wanted her dead. And with some luck, she might find the person responsible for sending the assassins.

'I agree with Gronk,' came another voice. This one was husky, as if it was trying too hard to be mysterious. Definitely a thief. 'And they're much faster, almost as if they're... *ex-adventurers*. I can't possibly sneak past them. It's no fun at all.'

'You too?' Panella whined. 'What can I tell you, Blade? I don't know why it's all zombies. I didn't raise them.'

'Adventuring not same no more,' said Gronk. 'I want good old days.'

'Well, they're gone,' snapped Panella. 'So get used to it.'

'Now it's all permits, limits and zombies,' said Blade. 'It completely saps the excitement out of things. How am I supposed to break the law when it's all declared and certified?'

'And no Elixir,' said Gronk.

'And no Elixir,' Blade agreed.

'The lack of Elixir is a bit of a blow,' Panella conceded. 'But we found some bottles here, didn't we?'

'They stale,' said Gronk. 'Not same.'

'Well, you shouldn't have gulped all of yours down in one go,' said Panella.

'It stop my shakes. I need.'

'We all need it,' said Panella. 'That's why we *must* ration ourselves and not glug them all at once like some greedy child…'

Xenixala ignored the rest of their blathering and turned a corner. The mine shaft opened into a larger room. It was full of rusted mining machinery. Ruined carts lay across the floor, and the walls were lined with shelves stacked with tools covered in cobwebs.

It was also surprisingly busy.

Hundreds of zombies levelled their gaze at Xenixala.

She froze.

That was a lot of zombies, even for her. These seemed different, though. They carried swords for one thing, also they moved with purpose. It was as if they could *understand*, which was quite uncharacteristic for a zombie. Xenixala shuddered.

She steadied herself for the onslaught and muttered an anti-undead charm. A wave of warmth flushed through her, which was expected. What wasn't expected, however, was the nausea. She steadied herself against a beam and retched as her whole body convulsed with fire. She quickly dispelled the charm, after which the feeling subsided.

Of course, she was undead. Using an anti-undead charm was probably the stupidest thing she could have done. At least no one was around to see… aside from the zombies.

Yet none had moved a muscle.

She was undead. She was one of them.

She was already immune.

That would be one less thing to worry about, at least.

Carefully, she walked into the mass of bodies. They shambled out of her way, which made her feel a tingle of power. Did the undead have some kind of unspoken mutual respect? It wasn't as if she could ask them.

In any case, they were not her concern. Xenixala continued following the voices and soon found the three of them hunched over a dead body, rifling through its shirt.

'There must be more in there,' said Blade. 'Keep digging! I need an Elixir. I need it *now*.'

'There nothing,' said Gronk, pulling up his hand, bringing the corpse's intestines with it. 'Just blood. And rusty dagger.'

'Bah!' exclaimed Blade. 'Zombies never have any good loot.' Blade had the classic appearance of a thief. He'd clearly bought his black cloak and black leather hide from the same shop as all the other pompous sorts who enjoyed crouching in shadows. Even though everyone knew it was there, the shop in question lay hidden in the Porkhaven sewers. Xenixala also knew the exact sales trick the grizzly shopkeeper played: he told the thieves that wearing leather hide allowed you to hide better, despite providing very limited protection at all.

Blade turned and saw Xenixala. 'Argh!' he leapt back. 'I mean, hah, I knew you were there, demon. Prepare to meet my *blade*.'

Xenixala rolled her eyes. 'Because you're called Blade. Very good.'

Panella and Gronk froze when they saw her.

'Xenixala...' said Panella, 'I can't believe... You look... well.' Panella's once blonde hair was now grey, her once fresh face now wrinkled in all the frowny areas. Stale and fresh blood spatters covered her clerics faded white surcoat. She looked at Xenixala with a darkened expression. Her hand moved to the mace on her belt.

Gronk simply grunted in her direction, which was more than he had usually said to her. She'd heard him talk most when he'd recited his poetry one night around the campfire. It was mainly about ways to smash a skull with an axe and rudimentary descriptions of flowers. Unsurprisingly, for a barbarian, he was more muscle than human. His clothing had been designed to express that—if you could call it clothing—as it consisted of only boots and a single loincloth. His hands tightened around his weapon, a great axe that probably weighed as much as he did.

'It's certainly been a while,' said Xenixala. 'I haven't had the pleasure of meeting Blade, however.'

Blade had flattened himself against the sheer cavern wall in an idiotic attempt to hide in an empty corridor. He locked eyes with Xenixala, then gave up and stepped forward. 'I am Sedrick The Blade, Half-Elf and Shadow in the Night, Keeper of...'

Xenixala cut him off. 'Yes, yes, I don't care. Half-elf, you don't say?'

'I do say. My mother was from Elfenvale, immortal and fair.'

'Ah, so you must be half mortal... Which half is it?'

Panella interjected, '*Don't* tell h...'

'My legs,' said Blade proudly.

Panella groaned. 'You're not supposed to *tell* people.'
'Why not? It's my heritage.'
'And your *weakness*.'
Blade tutted. 'As if my enemies can find me. I am but a shadow in…'
'In the night,' Xenixala finished. He was just as arrogant as all the other thieves. They thought cowardly hiding behind people and shooting a few arrows made them the most important members of an adventuring party when, in reality, they were the least. 'Don't worry, you have nothing to fear from me. I came here… to apologise.'
The adventurer's mouths gaped.
After a moment, Panella shook her head and laughed. 'The Great Xenixala of Xendor wants to *apologise* to us? After what you did?'
'Well, yes. I'm sorry. I didn't mean to ruin our party, turn everyone to stone and steal all the loot.' She pulled a slip of paper from her robes and read it. 'For my wrongs, please accept my sincerest apologies and inform me of any way I can make things right.'
Gronk growled.
'I agree with Gronk,' said Panella. 'What you did to us was unforgivable. We have only just financially recovered. Leave us be, *witch*.'
'*Listen*,' said Xenixala through gritted teeth. 'I'm trying to be a better person here. Accept my apology, and then I'll leave.'
'Never.'
Xenixala sighed. This was hopeless. Nobody wanted to make amends with her, and everyone that she had spoken to had been equally resentful. At this rate, she was never going to find whoever wanted her dead, so her reputation would forever be in the gutter.
'Wait a moment,' said Panella, sniffing the air. 'Are you… undead?'
'I uh…' said Xenixala, scratching the back of her neck. 'I maybe had a little transformation, yes.'
'You're… a vampire!' said Panella, drawing her sword. 'By all that is Holy, the undead shall be purged from this land!'
The other two adventurers drew their weapons in unison.
'Let me explain…' Xenixala began.
Panella lunged.
Xenixala leapt to the side as Panella thrust her mace in one fluid motion. She was surprisingly fast, but Xenixala was faster.
Gronk swung his axe down, but Xenixala was ready for the oaf's slow, predictable movements. She brought her nails down along his back, cutting deep. They were nails no longer—they were claws.

Gronk screamed a high-pitched wail and fell back. Regaining his composure, he said in a much lower pitch, 'I mean, ow.'

Blade had returned to pressing himself into the wall and took aim with his short bow.

A prickle of pain hit Xenixala's shoulder. She pulled the arrow out and tossed it to the floor. Snarling, she turned her attention to Blade. He gulped and shimmied along the wall towards a slightly darker shadow.

She was on Blade before he had time to pull out his namesake.

She aimed for his mortal legs. His blood sprayed across her. The delicious nectar coated her lips; the taste fuelled her frenzy. She spun to face Panella as Blade slumped to the floor.

Panella smiled as she brandished her mace to and fro. 'I've been waiting a long time for this, *witch*.'

'Likewise,' said Xenixala, licking her fingers of blood. It tasted sneaky.

Gronk had produced an entire wheel of cheese from somewhere and started to eat it furiously. Xenixala found herself frozen by the bizarre behaviour. It transfixed her so much that she couldn't keep her eyes off him. Once he was done with the giant cheese wheel, he ate seven apples, five pies, three blue potions and eight loaves of bread.

Gronk burped. His bleeding shoulders sparkled with light. Then, it was like he had never been cut at all. He stretched and picked up his axe.

Xenixala shook her head out of the trance. Food must have some kind of healing properties she had not considered. Without Elixir, adventurers must have been experimenting with alternatives.

No matter. She would not give him the chance to eat his way out again.

Xenixala bounded at them, teeth bared.

Panella swung her weapon, but Xenixala ducked under and struck at Gronk.

Gronk parried with the hilt of his axe, bellowing a war cry. His eyes went red as he spun with fury.

Xenixala leapt over the swipes, drilling into his head with her claws.

Gronk collapsed.

The cave shook as he landed, making grit fall from the ceiling. Hissing and groans replied in the distance.

Panella wiped the dust from her face and grimaced. 'Why is it that every time you appear, our lives are *ruined*?'

'It's *your* fault. I was *trying* to apologise.'

'I would nev...'

Panella shrieked.

Blade clawed into her back, biting her neck, his eyes white and mindless. Panella fell, and Blade tore at her until the screams stopped.

He'd become a zombie.

Gronk slowly stood. His eyes were pale too, face expressionless and covered with blood.

How could this be so? Adventurers don't turn into zombies. It wasn't possible.

At least it saved her some trouble.

'Maybe being a minion isn't so bad after all, eh Wordsworth?'

There was silence, except for the groans of three newly formed zombies.

'Wordsworth?'

When had she last seen Wordsworth?

13

Eric couldn't believe his eyes. At the top of the stairs was a lavish banquet room with a long dining table running down the middle. A dozen zombies sat around it, each dressed in ill-fitting, clean, formal attire: fancy hats, suits, frocks, cravats and dresses, all the latest fashion at court. The silverware on the table had been neatly arranged for a feast. However, upon closer inspection, the plates were heaped with red, oozing piles. Flies circulated the room with greedy buzzing. Some zombies lazily looked up at them, while others were face down on the plates. None got up to attack. Eric noticed then that they had been chained to their chairs.

Rose looked at Eric with concern. 'What... is this?'

'I have no idea,' said Eric. 'But it's giving me the creeps.'

A man appeared through a side door dressed in a loose, purple gown open down the front, revealing a pale, lithe frame. 'Who's for a little more tea?' he announced to the room without spotting Eric and Rose. 'Mrs Hagershall, now, I do know how much you *adore* your tea! How about another cup to wash down that dessert?'

Eric cleared his throat.

The man dropped his teapot, which shattered on the ground. 'Good grief!' he squealed. 'Please don't kill me! I've got so much left to die for!'

Eric raised his crossbow at the man. 'That's still undecided. Are you Steven?'

The man pushed back the greasy black hair under his patterned skullcap. 'With a V, or with a P?'

'Either.'

'Ah, then yes.' Steven sheepishly closed his robe. 'Are you here about the smell?'

'I'm afraid it's a bit more complicated than that.'

A zombie dressed in a black suit shambled into the room, holding a tray.

Steven took something from the tray and popped it in his mouth. 'Would either of you care for a mint?'

Eric and Rose both shook their heads.

'Suit yourself,' said Steven, dropping onto a red sofa. He raised one knee and looked up at them. 'How did you manage to sneak past my army so fast? You must be very well trained in the art of shadows.'

'We killed them all,' said Eric.

Steven's face crumbled. 'You... killed my beauties...' A tear ran down his cheek. 'But... how? They should... they should stop even the heartiest adventurers!'

Eric felt a pang of pity for the man. 'Oh, uh… it was very hard. They put up an excellent fight. Didn't they, Rose?'

'Um, yes, that's right,' said Rose. 'And no rope used at all, no siree.'

Eric lowered his crossbow. 'We're just very experienced. Don't beat yourself up about it.'

Steven wiped his cheeks and sat up. 'It's okay, I suppose. Plenty more where they came from. So what can I do for you? I'm afraid I don't have any treasure prepared, and I can't put up much of a fight. No one ever gets this far.'

'We're not here for that… we're not actually adventurers.'

'Oh, that's a relief,' said Steven. 'I can't stand those ruffians. They do leave such a mess. The char from fireball stains is a nightmare to rub out.'

Eric thought back to all sixteen floors they had passed, the piles of corpses and the endless splatters. 'They are a messy bunch.'

'Although,' said Steven, 'I haven't had to deal with many adventurers since The King got involved. It's been a blessed relief. I can *finally* enjoy myself in peace.'

Eric shuddered at the image of what this man might get up to with his corpses. He resisted the urge to shoot him right there and then. They needed answers. 'There's a new kind of zombie we're investigating, an *adventurer* zombie. Know anything about that?'

Steven frowned. 'Don't be silly. Adventurers can't become zombies. It's impossible. Too many resurrections and too much Elixir… don't think I haven't tried.'

'Well, it's what we saw. So explain that.'

Steven sniffed the air, his rodent-like nose wrinkled as he flitted his head back and forth. He looked down at Eric's ankle. 'You've been bitten!'

Eric shuffled onto his good leg. 'That's why we're on a bit of a deadline.'

Steven got up and crouched beside Eric's leg. His spine curved so much you could see the bones through his robe. He breathed in deeply, then sighed. 'This is a bad one. The only cure is to defeat the necromancer who raised the zombie who bit you.'

'Yes, yes, we know. We thought it was you… If I'm honest, the jury's still out on that one.'

Steven gulped. 'I… I… I don't know what to say. I keep all my pretties in the tower. If you got bit on your way up, that's your own fault.' Steven pulled up Eric's trouser leg and winched. 'This wound is far too old for that, though.'

The wound throbbed even harder than before. 'How long have I got?'

'Hard to say, especially if this is a new zombie breed. You're likely to turn at the most dramatic or ironic point…' Steven stood up and paused for effect, narrowing his eyes at Eric. Once it was clear

Eric wasn't about to zombify, he continued. 'Curses like this *love* irony. It could be in two minutes or two weeks. I guess it will be the latter, as you've already lasted this long...' Steven kept looking at Eric.

'I'm not turning any time soon,' said Eric with a huff. 'I've been using all the anti-undead charms I can think of.'

'Ah,' said Steven. 'That explains it. Have you tried eggs, too?'

'Eggs?'

'Indeed. Lather the wound with egg yolk. It's an *excellent* undead preventative.'

Eric was sure Steven had emphasised the first syllable of "excellent" to sound like "egg". 'So how does that work?'

'It is new life!' said Steven, waving his hand theatrically. 'It is the perfect counter to un-life.'

'That doesn't make any sense,' said Rose. 'You'll be killing the egg... so wouldn't that just be more death?'

Steven scoffed. 'I don't make the rules.'

'Fine,' said Eric, making a mental note to update his shopping list. 'No harm in trying. But how can you prove you're not the one making these new zombies? What is it that you do up here, exactly?'

'So many glorious things!' Steven spoke faster, like a child about to tell you about a stick they had found, as if they were the first person ever to have found a stick. 'Come this way...'

Steven led them through a side door onto a darkened gangway suspended from the ceiling with chains. It overlooked an illuminated maze of rooms and corridors, with various mock-up dungeons filled with cheap furniture and painted-on cave wall texture.

'This is my training centre!' explained Steven with glee. 'My life's work.'

They walked onto the gangway, which swayed with their steps. Eric drew breath when he saw the forms wandering the rooms below. They were littered with zombies. He pushed the peg further onto his nostrils. Seeing the world from above like this must be what being a god would feel like.

Steven drew a deep breath and sighed. 'My pretties aren't easy things to control, you know. They need the necessary skills to take on adventurers. Otherwise, they would be totally aimless. Training these beauties takes a lot of time and dedication.'

'I'm sure,' said Eric. None of the zombies moved faster than a bored tortoise. These were clearly not the adventuring kind.

'The hardest part is making them go solo,' said Steven. 'They don't do so well away from the crowd. Observe.' Steven pointed to a single zombie slowly descending one of the corridors, which had been painted to look like a mine shaft. At the end was a scarecrow that had been given a helmet and plate armour covered in what appeared to be pork chops.

'See how quietly Susan moves!' said Steven in a whisper, 'She'll sneak right up to the adventurer and strike.'

Eric had never considered it, but now it made so much sense. Zombies usually make so much hissing and grunting that you would expect to hear them coming a mile away. But sometimes, they catch you off guard and seem to appear out of thin air.

The zombie reached the scarecrow and lunged, ripping into it with its teeth. Straw and scraps of pork flew into the air.

Steven clapped with joy. 'I think Susan might be ready!'

Eric then noticed that the fake dungeons below had an unsettling number of beds. He shuddered. If Steven had to go through all this trouble to make his zombies walk right, there was no way he would have made the fast, armoured adventurer undead they had faced.

'Alright,' said Eric. 'So maybe you're not the necromancer we're after. But perhaps you can tell us where we could find him or her. Do you know of any other suspicious necromancers?'

'I don't know any, I'm afraid,' said Steven, not taking his eyes off Susan, the zombie. 'We're a solitary bunch. Very hard to keep track of your minions when there's another lot mixed in with them. Have you tried asking the undead?'

Eric frowned. 'And how are we supposed to do that?'

'Why, a seance, of course.'

Eric's patience grew thin. 'What in The Mole's name do you mean? We're not looking for ghosts.'

Steven laughed without smiling, which had a most unsettling effect. 'A zombie is just a cursed dead body. Their spirit is trapped somewhere in The Underworld. If you speak with them, they'll know where their body is and what happened to it. The dead are quite attached to their bodies, although not literally, of course.'

'And how are we supposed to find a cursed soul trapped in The Underworld?'

Steven pointed to Eric's leg. 'The curse is in your veins now. A mystic could find a soul bound to the curse with a drop of your blood.'

Rose looked at Eric. 'Good job that you got bitten then, I suppose.'

'All things considered.' Eric stroked his greying stubble. 'In fact, I know a mystic in Porkhaven who owes me a favour.'

Rose jumped up and down. 'Let's get going then!'

Steven smiled. 'Glad to be of service! While you're there... do let me know if you see any graveyards that look a little... full.'

'Sure thing,' said Eric as he pulled a Scroll of Town Portal from his bag.

Soon, The King's guard will work double shifts at all graveyards within a ten-mile radius. Eric will ensure it.

14

The Lady Enchantress Xenixala of Xendor, Yielder of Grain, Empress of Time and author of *"How I Made My Millions With Toads And One Simple Trick"* rolled over in her bed and groaned. The sounds of Porkhaven's streets clamoured in her ears. It was as if the denizens were in her skull, shouting about how cheap their wares were, coughing, spitting, screaming, and moaning about the weather.

Her vampire senses were strong. Too strong.

She threw back the covers, got up, and began pacing in the sorry excuse for a room she had found herself. She'd almost caught the sunrise that morning, which would have been somewhat fatal had she not dashed into the nearest Inn. The innkeeper had been most confused when she asked for a room for the *day*. They only had night rates, which meant she'd had to pay for two nights instead of one. It was, quite literally, daylight robbery.

She cursed as a beam of light burst through the window and seared her skin. The interminable sun was trying its best to creep in through the cracks in the curtains. She hauled the shabby cupboard across the floorboards and over to the window, then threw herself back onto the flea-ridden bed and closed her eyes.

Now she understood why vampires liked black and red so much. They were the only colours that didn't dig into her irises to look at. This wasn't a huge problem when confined to the darkness of the night, but it would be nice to have some wardrobe flexibility. Vampires enjoying red made sense when you thought about it. An aversion to the colour of blood would cut off their only source of food.

She thought of something to say but realised again that she was alone. As much as she hated to admit it, she missed Wordsworth.

How could she have been so stupid? Of course, he would have disappeared. He was her familiar, an extension of her soul. The curse took her soul. After all, she was technically dead.

Who was she going to complain to now? She kept making witty remarks, but no one was around to hear them. It was awful.

And there was the emptiness.

It was like drinking a watered-down, low-alcohol ale. It didn't have the same zest, zing, and pizazz as it should. And now life didn't either. Everything was just "meh." She thought she'd felt "meh" about life before and didn't think it could get any worse. She'd taken the innate spark inside her for granted. Even if it had been dull, it was still there.

Now, there was nothing.

All that was left was a great void that could never be filled.

All that was left was the thirst.

No matter who she hunted or how much blood she drank. Nothing.

She did try to quench the painful hunger with expensive wine and what should have been a delightful duck confit, but that just made her vomit so violently that she had ruined the ceiling of the restaurant. She could never eat food again. Nor get drunk. And those were some of her top five things to do.

Only blood satisfied her now. The hunger sat in the pit of her stomach, a caged beast that endlessly demanded more.

Now, whenever she encountered a living creature, she had to resist the urge to rip it to shreds and bathe in its entrails. This involved biting her lip, and that taste only worsened things. How was she supposed to get her reputation back on track with these urges?

The poor innkeeper downstairs never saw it coming. Maybe he shouldn't have charged extra.

The guards would indeed be called soon, so what was she to do? She was trapped until nightfall. She had no one to talk to and nothing to do but dwell.

Worst of all, her room overlooked an old Adventurer's Supply shop, now rebranded to *"Sword's 'N Stuff"* and presumably privately owned after the Adventurer's Supply economic crash. Each time a new customer came into the shop, she heard the jingle of the infernal doorbell and every word of the chit-chat that ensued.

Xenixala pulled the pillow over her head and tried to get back to sleep.

Sure enough, the jingle chimed with a new customer—likely some kind of warrior, judging by the confident and heavy footsteps.

'I wish to sell you three hundred sixty-three iron daggers,' said the warrior, her voice firm. There was a colossal crash as she dropped the three hundred sixty-three metal things onto the countertop.

'Please,' the shopkeep whimpered. He had a high-pitched voice and was probably a gnome or other lowly creature. 'I physically cannot sell any more iron daggers. I'll be ruined!'

'The Sword's 'N Stuff guarantee states they will purchase *any* and *all* items.'

The shopkeep sighed. 'As you wish, adventurer.'

'I also have this bucket and an apple to sell. I need to free up space in my Sack of Clutching.' There was a rattle and a thud.

'That apple is completely rotten! How long have you had it in there?'

'I dunno, a few months.'

'A few *months*?! And you expect me to resell it? Who would *ever* buy that?'

The adventurer cleared her throat. 'You forget yourself shopkeep. *Any* and *all* items.'

'Urgh, fine. At least I can *maybe* sell that bucket... wait.' There was a pause. 'This is *my* bucket! You took this from behind the shop!'

'No, I didn't.'

'Look, it has my initials on it!'

'That could be anyone's initials.'

'Oh yeah, then where did you get it?'

'I found it behind a different shop.'

'Likely story, thief. What if I called the guard on you?'

The adventurer laughed. 'You think I care? My reputation is about as bad as it could be. Do you really want their blood all over your shop floor? Just because of a rusty bucket I didn't steal from behind your shop? And anyway, I'm part of the new Thieves Guild so I get a daily pass at getting caught.'

'So you expect me just to *buy* it back? My own bucket.'

There was a pause. 'Indeed. *Any* and *all* items.'

'Well, fine. But you're only getting one copper piece for each one. That's the lowest I can go because that's the smallest piece of currency.'

'Excellent. With my three hundred and sixty-five copper pieces... I would like to buy an enchanted item. What do you have?'

The shopkeeper spoke as if through gritted teeth. 'With what you can afford, *adventurer*, I have The Ring of Quietness, The Stone of Truth, The Breastplate of Hellfire, The Handbag of Endurance, or The Whisk of Undying.'

'The Whisk of Undying?' the adventurer tutted. 'Who enchanted that?'

'How am I supposed to know? An ancient witch or something, I suppose. Does it matter?'

'Just seems a little odd, that's all. The Handbag of Endurance? You're making these up.'

'Some other adventurer sold them to me, *and as you well know*, I cannot refuse. I don't know where they came from.'

'Adventurers don't use handbags.'

'Well, maybe they ran out of your normal things to enchant and only had kitchenware and accessories to hand. Does that help?'

'Not really.' There was a pause. 'I'll keep it safe and go with The Breastplate of Hellfire.'

The shopkeep laughed to himself. 'As you wish... *adventurer*. But be warned, this was stolen from the depths of The Underworld itself.' There was the sound of rustling and a box being opened. 'Here you are.'

'Hold on, there's nothing to this!'

'What do you mean? It has the finest protective properties.'

'Only for my chest! It's basically a bra.'

'Very economical with the fabric, perfect for travelling light.'

'I'll be freezing!'

'Adventurers spend so much time running around. This will help you cool down.'

'It'll barely protect my nipples. How is that supposed to help?'

'The two domes reverse the magnetic polarity of incoming steel, creating an aura of protection. Or two auras, rather.'

'Oh. Is that so?'

'Yeah, sure, why not.'

'Interesting... and you think it will suit me? Does it match my cloak?'

'Very much so. Blends perfectly with the rough aesthetic.'

'Very well,' said the warrior. 'You have yourself a deal, shopkeeper.'

'Thank you, adventurer. Have a *good* day.' The emphasis on "good" sounded sarcastic and subtle enough that no rational person would have said anything about it, but they would still feel insulted.

The door jingled again, and the bliss of silence resumed.

Xenixala rolled over again and sighed. She missed being an adventurer. Even the inane conversations with shopkeepers.

She missed the sunshine and people and wine and song and colours and life and everything.

And Wordsworth.

Those vampires had tricked her. They knew what the curse meant and let her have it anyway. She was supposed to be making herself stronger, not weaker.

Resolute, she smiled and stretched. As soon as the sun set, she would return to Castle Vanderblad and unleash hell. Those vampires needed to be stopped, and she could be the hero to stop them.

Vanderblad would regret ever hearing her name.

15

Skwee sat in front of a golden magic mirror, a notepad in one hand and Eric's glass of water in the other. The magic mirror sprung to life, and a logo flashed across the reflection. This lit up the tiny office he'd been assigned to, deep in the warrens of The New Master's lair. The logo was a skull with a golden crown, which spun as a cheery voice spoke:

'Welcome to the evil overlord training seminar, Part One of Six. Thank you for choosing Overlord Systems Inc. as your guide. Please remember to like, share, and subscribe. Simply ask at your local owlery.'

Skwee had seen the same seminar years ago as part of his training to assist The Dark Master, but the details had grown fuzzy. He'd told Edwardius about the seminars, who'd seemed delighted with the idea and found a magic mirror almost immediately. Skwee had hoped Edwardius would just do the training then let him go, but no such luck. He wanted Skwee to make notes and relay the information personally. Something about delegation being "the key to success".

If Skwee didn't help Edwardius become a successful evil overlord, it would be a pain worse than death. Or possibly even worse than that, which was about as bad as things could ever get.

The mirror continued:

'The first step to being an evil overlord is to have an evil master plan. You may find it helpful to have a brooding spot to assist with its creation. A brooding spot will help to clear your mind, allowing you to be filled with a sense of empowerment. This is why your lair must be dramatic, such as a ledge overlooking the city that wronged you, or maybe inside a volcano, or even a simple study with a crackling fireplace. You will know that your plan is evil enough once the thought of it makes you cackle and rub your hands together...'

Skwee scribbled furiously into his notepad with his quill. His last master had been a prolific brooder, but Skwee had always wondered if it had just been an excuse to drink more tea.

'Once you have an evil master plan,' continued the mirror, *'you must recruit minions. The best minions are persuadable creatures, such as goblins, orcs, kobolds or ogres who do not have a moral compass.'*

Skwee nodded sagely. He'd never owned a compass.

'If you do employ human minions, be sure they cover faces with a helmet or visor. Humans never want to look another human in the eye as they kill them. It makes them feel bad. Other species have no moral issue with killing as they are considered ugly. To a human, ugliness equates to evil.'

Humans were a funny lot, it was true. They acted as if they had moral superiority over other races, yet they were usually more ruthless and power-hungry than all the others combined. The fact that they held most positions of power was both terrifying and reassuring.

'Basic power structures for an evil overlord are also key to your success. Depending on the size of your minion army, it could be as simple as having you at the top and everyone else below you. However, delegation will become very important as your army grows. Find successful minions to promote and give them limited command powers.'

Skwee copied this down on his notebook, then crossed it out. Edwardius already knew that bit. He'd delegated this to him, after all.

'When these commanders disobey or fail you, be sure to kill them as brutally and quickly as possible. Do not let the other minions see weakness, as they might then revolt against you. This is especially true of messengers who bring bad news. They should be killed immediately, lest they pass the bad news amongst your ranks.'

Skwee smiled to himself. He had experienced his fair share of punishments from evil overlords, which had never been proportional. They were only doing their job, so he didn't really mind it.

'A good training program for your minions is also key to success. However, never train your army in ranged combat, as it wastes too much ammunition. This is a cost that is easily saved.'

This was also true. Everyone knew how expensive arrows were. They often cost more than the goblins themselves. However, this lack of training did mean that goblin archers rarely hit their enemies.

'Minion training procedures will be covered in more detail in Part Five. However, knowing The Hierarchy of Waste is an important ground rule. One example of The Hierarchy of Waste is constantly sending the lowest and most incompetent minions to do tasks first. They will not know the importance of their task and will, therefore, not betray you. Then, if they fail, you will send progressively more competent minions until the job is done.

'Likewise, send your weakest minions to fight the adventurers first, then send incrementally stronger ones until the adventurers are eventually defeated. This way, you will only ever lose the weakest of your minions, which allows you to determine the exact level required for any given task without committing a more valuable minion who may then over-deliver.'

Skwee scratched his head. It all seemed confusing. He'd always been sent in first to face the adventurers, so he wasn't sure what happened after they inevitably chopped him to pieces. He was just lucky to be resurrected.

'Each evil master plan will require specific needs, which we will cover in Part Three. However, they all follow the same basic structure. To begin, we recommend that you select a nemesis. Although not essential, having a nemesis will help motivate you to complete your goals. If you cannot think of a nemesis, you may discover one as you enact your evil master plan. Keep a watchful eye out for adventurers trying a little too hard to disrupt your evil master plan. They may also be looking for a nemesis, which is a role you could fulfil for them. Both parties will then motivate one another to greater success.'

Skwee had heard Edwardius complaining a lot about a witch who had apparently ruined his life. So he was already sorted on the nemesis front.

'You may find yourself face-to-face with your nemesis at some point in your evil master plan. It is vitally important that you do not kill them, as they are key to your continued motivation. Be sure to lock them up in a way that they can quite easily escape, then protract any executions with monologues until they realise that they can free themselves. If this fails, you can offer them freedom if they can beat you in a contest that appears impossible, but one that you have actually rigged in their favour. This could include chess, combat with unusual weapons or a riddle.'

Monologues were the worst. They usually made Skwee's eyes glaze over, and his mind would drift to images of delicious rat-pie. However, they seemed important, so he wrote and underlined it.

'The edge of a cliff, or similar high place, is perfect for a showdown with your nemesis. There are many ways to survive a fall, such as with magic or simple tricks like concealed mattresses. This will allow either of you to save face and still escape, as the other will assume you have died.'

Two of Skwee's past overlords had fallen to their deaths from a great height after a showdown with an adventurer. It only just occurred to him that maybe they hadn't died after all and had used their fall to abandon their minions and responsibilities.

'Another excellent way to goad your nemesis is to kidnap their beloved, or prince/princess, then force them to marry you. This should be done with a lavish wedding that takes weeks to prepare. This will give your kidnapped fiancé time in their cell to realise they do really love you after all, and also time for your nemesis to arrive. The marriage will strengthen your power in the land and further motivate you to complete your evil plan.'

It sounded like Edwardius was already infatuated with some kind of zombie pixie called Felina. So he didn't bother writing that one down.

'Setting up your lair for the impending invasion of your nemesis is vitally important. Be sure to hire an orchestra to hide in your brooding room. They will provide dramatic music to motivate you

and your nemesis to the most epic showdown possible. But again, remember, try not to kill them.

'In fact, hurting any adventurers can be very costly, as they will often take a lawsuit against you for making your lair unsafe. Use plenty of signage to warn of danger, and only employ traps in obvious places like doorways and treasure chests. A booby-trapped chair, for example, is a no-no.'

Skwee was glad that this rule was used in constructing evil lairs, as it meant he only occasionally found himself caught in his Master's traps. Otherwise, it would cost them a fortune in resurrections.

'In the design of your lair, always have plenty of hidden tunnels, secret exits and large ducts that are big enough to crawl through. That way, you can always escape in the unlikely event of a fire...'

Skwee yawned and closed his eyes for a moment. There was only so much listening he could endure.

'...and stay tuned for Part Two...'

He awoke with a start, nearly knocking over the glass of water.

'...where we will cover immortality using ancient artefacts, detailing how to effectively scatter them across the land...'

He rubbed his eyes. What time was it? How long had he been asleep?

'...but don't forget to mash that "like and subscribe" button...'

Hopefully, his notes should be enough.

'...it really helps spread the word of Overlord Systems Inc.'

Otherwise, according to said notes, it would be a fate worse than a fate worse than death.

16

Queen Warlock Xenixala of Xendor, Bringer of Hope, Dawn of Despair and owner of several unfurnished homesteads across the kingdom, kicked at the door of Castle Vanderblad, which splintered into a hundred pieces. She stalked into the hall within, her heart racing.

'*Where are you, Vanderblad*?' she screeched into the darkness. She could see perfectly despite the lack of light. What she saw stopped her dead in her tracks.

The great hall was packed full of people. Was it some kind of party? There was barely room to move for bodies.

Not people.

Zombies.

The horde shambled around, groaning. Some were adventurers, some were townsfolk, and some were the vampire's familiars. Despite being undead, the familiars still mopped the floor, only now in a less coordinated fashion. As they moved, their rotting flesh oozed onto the ground, which they turned to mop up, making more ooze. An endless cycle of cleaning. It was probably a pretty similar existence to what they had before.

The castle doorman, Eyegore, was among them too. His face was still somewhat toad-like, but now rotted, with skin flapping down in ways it shouldn't. Flies buzzed everywhere.

Xenixala put a hand over her nose. The stench was almost unbearable. How could they live like this? Had the vampires left?

She shoved the zombies aside, who mulched out of her way as she strode further into the great hall.

'I know you're in here, Vanderblad,' she called out. 'I can *smell* you.'

She periodically sniffed to follow the scent, which made her retch and return to holding her breath.

She reached the end of the hall to the raised dais, on top of which was a tremendous bat-shaped chair. Lady Vanderblad sat, looking down at the mass of bodies, a bored expression on her face. A thin, blood-red crown held her white hair together. Before, her hair had seemed perfect, almost as if it had been made of marble, but now it tangled as if she'd just woken up.

'I wondered when you would return,' said Lady Vanderblad with a smile. 'It took you a lot longer than the others.'

'*You,*' Xenixala spat. '*You* did this to me.'

Lady Vanderblad tutted. 'I only did as you asked.'

The zombies continued their groans.

'You didn't tell me what it was like,' said Xenixala. 'You lied.'

'I said nothing. You did this to yourself. I did only as you wished.'

Xenixala shook with rage. 'You didn't tell me how bad it was. It's awful! I can't eat, or drink, or feel or anything. And you *knew* that.'

Lady Vanderblad grinned, revealing her pointed teeth. 'It's what you deserve.'

'See?' Xenixala exclaimed. 'You *did* trick me. You knew the downsides and *conveniently* didn't mention it. Lying by omission is still lying.'

Lady Vanderblad rolled her eyes. 'I do not care to debate semantics. What's done is done. Every vampire goes through the same phase. They always complain. But it will pass.'

'This will never pass. How can *anyone* live like this?'

Lady Vanderblad gestured to the other vampires lounging in the corner. The zombies milled around them, paying no attention. 'We manage just fine.'

The vampires looked like husks that could be mistaken for furniture. Barely moving a muscle, their ivory faces were sullen and lifeless.

'Hardly!' Xenixala snorted. 'Look at this mess. You can't move for zombies in here. This castle is a state at the best of times. But this is something else.'

Lady Vanderblad sighed. 'I tried to get some Pest Control in, but they still haven't replied to my letter.'

Xenixala thought back to Eric and his feeble friends. 'Pest Control are a waste of time. Do it yourself.'

'It's just... not the same when the prey is already dead.'

Xenixala knew precisely what she meant but didn't want to give her the satisfaction. 'You live in filth, and you don't even leave this wretched castle. I don't want your pitiful existence. I want the cure. So tell it to me, or I'll rip your throat out.'

Lady Vanderblad rolled her head back and laughed, long and deep. 'You will not like it. Nobody does.'

'I'll be the judge of that. Tell me. Now.'

'Very well.' Lady Vanderblad sat upright and licked her lips. 'There are only two cures for the vampire's curse. One way...' she paused for effect, 'is true love's kiss.'

It was Xenixala's turn to laugh. A cold, heartless laugh. She shook her head at the audacity. 'You can't be serious? *True love's kiss*? Like in the children's stories? You must be joking.'

'Do I look like someone who jokes?'

'How am I supposed to fall in love without a soul? I couldn't even do that as a human, let alone now. It's impossible.'

Xenixala had never even remotely had a boyfriend. Sure, she'd had plenty of suitors, but after more than about a week, they became too much of a bore. Something about their neediness churned her stomach. Having a companion in her bed for a night was much more straightforward. Any more than that, and you can't get rid of them.

'I said you wouldn't like it,' said Lady Vanderblad.

'Has anyone *ever* managed that?'

'Not that I know of.'

Xenixala groaned. 'Ok, fine. What's the other way?'

'The other way?'

'You said there were two ways.'

'Ah, yes... but I suspect you won't like that either.'

Xenixala gritted her teeth. '*Tell me.*'

The hum of zombie moans floated through the air while they stared at one another.

Lady Vanderblad sighed. 'You simply... have to get your soul back.'

Xenixala frowned. 'My soul? Where even is it?'

'Where else do dead souls go? The afterlife, of course. Or at least the part before the afterlife that allows *cursed* souls to dwell... *The Underworld.*'

Xenixala pushed back the terrifying thoughts of existential dread. 'You're telling me the afterlife is real?'

'I wouldn't know, for I have not been. Nor do I know of anyone who has. It's only what is said.'

Xenixala had, in fact, been to The Underworld on two separate occasions. Once for business and once for pleasure. Both times had been disappointing, mainly on account of it being a relentless hellscape of lava and demons. However, the souvenirs were fabulous. They had the best treasure down there, even if half of it melted your skin. Everything had a fun name like: 'The Hellsword of Widowflesh', or 'Bloodletter of Anguish'. And if there was one thing Xenixala enjoyed, it was dramatic names. However, she wasn't aware that The Underworld counted as the afterlife. She thought it was just where evil came from—and sometimes lawyers.

'I have to go to The Underworld?' said Xenixala. 'No big deal.'

'It's not so simple,' Lady Vanderblad scoffed. 'You must enter The Underworld after death, as you pass to the afterlife. The Underworld is a net that catches many lost souls as they pass on. Your soul will be hidden in the part of The Underworld where only death belongs.'

'Let me get this straight. I have to die, then go to The Underworld and *then* come back with my soul?'

Lady Vanderblad smiled again. She was relishing in this far too much. 'Indeed. But if you die as a vampire, you become nothing. Your soul is already gone.'

Xenixala rubbed her temples. This was going nowhere. 'So how do you expect me to go to the afterlife?'

'You cannot. I did say you wouldn't like it.'

'It sounds like this curse is being intentionally annoying.'

'It wouldn't be much of a curse otherwise, would it?'

Xenixala couldn't believe the absurdity. Maybe Vanderblad was just toying with her.

'How do I know I can trust what you're saying is true?'

'You cannot. But I am telling you the truth. Ask any other vampire, and they will tell you the same.'

Now that Xenixala thought about it, every vampire she had ever met had been anaemic, forlorn and apathetic. How could she have been so blind? They were wretched creatures, and she had been a fool to want to become one. Sure, there was tremendous power, but it came at the cost of being a mopey loser in a crumbling castle full of zombies.

Lady Vanderblad reached out and beckoned with her finger. 'Forget about your soul. It is a worthless appendage; you are better off without its burden. Instead, why not *join* our coven? Every vampire I have ever turned returns here. They always ask for the cure, they always ask the same questions, but then they always stay.'

Xenixala frowned. There were worse ways to live. At Castle Vanderblad she would have a ready supply of blood, the safety of darkness and like-minded companions.

But she couldn't allow herself to slip into their apathy, even though her very essence drew her to it. Was this some kind of spell? She had to focus.

Xenixala shook her head, resolved. 'No deal. I will find this cure, even if it kills me—which seems like a requisite.'

'Very well.' Lady Vanderblad raised a single eyebrow. 'I wish you luck. You'll need it.'

Xenixala clenched her fists. She would love nothing more than to scratch the smug expression off her pallid face. She could tear them apart—all the vampires and all the zombies—leaving them as just a pool of blood.

She looked over at the miserable vampires lying on the ground.

They were already living in hell. There was no pain worse that she could inflict on them. An eternity of their pathetic life was punishment enough.

Knowing this, she turned and left Castle Vanderblad, vowing never to return.

17

Eric mopped his brow with a handkerchief and rapped the wooden door with a shaking fist. The mystic's shack was deep in Porkhaven's Wizard's District, with air that had the unmistakable tang of magic. It made him think of almonds mixed with copper. The shack looked like it had been built in an afternoon, yet had somehow managed to survive for a hundred years. Blankets of moss coated the wonky walls, and light beamed out from the cracks of the poor woodsmanship, which illuminated the porch against the dark of the night. Mystics refused to open during sociable hours, claiming they needed the moon to do their work. In reality, they spent the daylight hours hungover from ingesting too many hallucinogens the night before.

Eric wiped the sweat from his face again, trying to turn away from Rose so she wouldn't see. Everything felt hot and cold at the same time. The zombie bite on his leg throbbed with each heartbeat. Every time he moved, a sharp burning sensation shot through his body. Whenever he thought of the pain, an urge swelled inside of him. A whisper told him to give in, to stop fighting. To eat brains. He took a breath and pushed the feelings back down.

He hoped Skwee was alright. They hadn't seen him in quite some time, which was most unusual for a goblin with his kind of loyalty. He must have got lost chasing a rat or something. If he still wasn't there once they returned to the shop, he'd put up some *'Lost: Goblin'* posters around the neighbourhood.

The mystic's door swung open to reveal a wrinkled woman hunched over and wrapped in rags. She craned her neck up at them and smiled.

'Ah, Eric, I knew it was you,' said Mystic Mogg through a toothless grin. 'Do come in.'

Mystics had an annoying habit of acting like they knew about something before it happened. Yet, they would conveniently only tell you about their alleged prediction after seeing the outcome.

Eric and Rose exchanged glances and followed Mystic Mogg into her house. Eric held his breath to hide the agony of each step.

The inside of the shack was a mess of oddities, skulls and crystals. The aroma of herbal concoctions hung heavily in the air, occasionally wrestling with the scent of musty incense. A pack of tarot cards quietly played poker with a glowing runestone on a side table, while strings of hanging bones gently clattered overhead.

There were also far fewer shrunken heads than he had expected.

'I suppose you've noticed that I've cut down on the shrunken heads,' said Mystic Mogg as she hobbled over to her chair. A mouse scuttled out of her path and disappeared behind a bucket of glass eyes.

'Oh, really?' said Eric, feigning surprise.

'Weren't good for business,' she grunted. 'I never wanted that many, mind you. But these things happen. No one knows what to buy you; then, one person gives you a shrunken head, and someone sees it and then gets you one, too. Then you're known as "the shrunken head lover", and that's all you'll ever be given. Before you know it, you have a whole roomful.'

'I see.'

Mystic Mog gestured to the table in the centre of the room. 'Please take a seat.'

Eric plopped into the chair and breathed a sigh of relief. Rose and Mystic Mogg joined him.

'I'm afraid this isn't a social call…' said Eric.

'Please try to be quiet,' said Mystic Mogg in a hushed tone, gesturing to the curtains at the back. 'I have a customer in the other room on a, uh, *journey*.'

Most mystics' customers were people pretending they wanted to see into the future, but it was just a cheap way to escape reality for a few hours.

Eric lowered his voice, 'I'm afraid this isn't a social call, I… *we*, need your help.'

'I see,' said Mystic Mogg, sitting back in her chair, which creaked in complaint. 'I'll do what I can, as it's you. The recent batch of soul stones have been *most* useful.'

They had a long-standing arrangement in which Eric informed her of any establishments infested with ghosts, spirits, or poltergeists he couldn't manage on his own. Eric never asked her what she did with the souls she trapped. He suspected he was better off never knowing.

'A zombie has bitten me, and we need to find the necromancer who created the curse. If we stop them, I might be cured.'

Mystic Mogg looked him up and down. 'You are in the later stages of your transformation. You don't have long.'

'You think I don't know that?' Eric coughed weakly. 'We've heard that if we can speak to the spirits of those infected by the curse, they could point us to the necromancer responsible.'

Mystic Mogg furrowed her brow. 'Talking to the dead would require a seance. Lucky for you, I've just had a fresh shipment of genies come in. If the curse is in your blood, the genie will be able to find the way. But this is no light matter. Is your mind ready for such a thing?'

'I'll try anything once,' Eric muttered. 'Although it's not like I have much choice.'

Mystic Mogg nodded gravely. 'Then we shall proceed,' she said, standing up with a pace that suggested her bones preferred she lay down. She went over to a drawer and produced a wooden slab and a glass tumbler, which she placed at the centre of the table. On the slab were a series of runes and symbols.

'Is that a Wee Genie Board?' asked Rose, her eyes wide with excitement.

'It is,' said Mystic Mogg. She took a crystal from her pocket and put it inside the upturned glass tumbler on the board. She whispered an incantation and the crystal throbbed blue. 'The genie in the crystal will only last a short time,' she said. 'Eric, give me your finger.'

Eric complied. With surprising swiftness, a dagger appeared in her hand. She thrust it across Eric's forefinger.

He yelped as blood oozed.

Mystic Mogg grabbed his hand and pushed the bloody finger onto the tumbler.

'How will I know what to do?' Eric stammered.

'Oh, you'll know…' said Mystic Mogg.

Then, there was only darkness.

'Hello?' Eric called out into the void. He looked down at himself, but there was nothing there.

Groans whispered in the infinite emptiness.

'Hello?' he called out again, his voice faltering as it echoed. Strangely, the pain in his leg had gone, which made sense. He didn't seem to have a body.

He needed to focus. How do you move in a void? He pictured himself moving towards the groans. The noise grew. He pictured it even harder. The noises grew even more.

Soon, a wall of spirits stood shoulder to shoulder before him, glaring with vacant eyes. They glowed in the darkness, their transparent bodies melting and shimmering at the edges. Eric noticed they were lined up beside a great body of water, which disappeared into the darkness. Its waves silently lapped non-existent banks.

'Ah… uh… hello, spirits,' said Eric, smiling, uncertain if they could see his face. 'Nice to meet you.'

'Please save your lies,' said one of the spirits, who appeared to be a sort of ex-bard judging by the translucent lute in his arms. 'Everyone knows it's wretched here. And we look like *death*.'

The other spirits groaned in unison and clamoured various insults.

'Shut *up*, Rodger.'

'I wish I could kill you, Rodger.'

'Die again, please, Rodger.'

Rodger seemed undeterred. 'Please ignore my compatriots. We do grow a little *weary* being stuck down here.'

'And uh…' said Eric. 'Where is here, exactly?'

'Why, The Underworld, of course!' answered the spirit matter-of-factly. 'We cannot pass through here and into the afterlife while our mortal forms are kept in that *horrid* state.'

'You mean as zombies?'

The spirit seemed to shudder. 'Why, indeed. That ghastly curse! We are all still rather attached to our earthly bodies—quite *literally*, of course.'

The other spirits groaned again.

Rodger ignored them and continued, 'Our bodies are not entirely dead, so *He Who Sails* won't allow passage across The Sea of Souls. We are trapped. Until the curse is lifted, we cannot enter the afterlife, whatever that will be.'

Eric was stunned that all the Holy Mole sermons he'd been forced to attend as a child had been right about an afterlife, although they had never mentioned a "He Who Sails" or a "Sea of Souls." It all seemed oddly nautical. Everyone knew an Underworld existed, but nobody thought it led to an afterlife. It was just the place where evil came from—and sometimes lawyers.

'We're adventurers, for goodness sake,' said Rodger. 'We shouldn't be able to become undead. It's an outrage. Now our lovely, handsome bodies are being dragged about the land, stinking and dripping everywhere. It's such an embarrassment.'

'Well then,' said Eric. 'You may be in luck; I'm actually trying to stop the very necromancer in question. But I'll need your help.'

There was a murmur of agreement amongst the spirits.

Rodger nodded. 'Then you should speak with *her*. Follow me.'

The spirits parted, creating a tunnel of bodies. Rodger led Eric through the mass of spirits, each looking at him with eager eyes. Eric couldn't believe how many there were. Countless souls trapped and bound.

Eventually, the pathway of ghosts ended, encircling one tiny figure in the centre. She was less ethereal than the others, almost as if she was halfway to being physical.

'Hello,' said the figure. 'You look like you don't belong here… yet.' She was small and pointy, a pixie with long blond hair and a kind face.

Eric tried to clear his throat, even though it didn't exist. 'I don't have long. Who are you?'

'I'm Felina,' she said, gesturing to the spirits floating around them. 'I am the source of all their pain. I've been watching you, Eric. I can feel my curse inside of you. I have kept it at bay but can't continue for much longer.'

'I appreciate that.'

'For you see,' she said sadly. 'My blood made the curse. I was the key. The key that my beloved used to spread this death. This unlife. He is to blame.'

'Who is he?' Eric spoke quickly. 'Your beloved. Who is he, and where can we find him?'

'All of us can feel our bodies still trapped in the mortal realm, and I can feel mine beside him. He is hidden in the heart of Porkhaven. I know not where, but I may be able to guide you when the time comes.'

Eric felt a force pull him from within. 'Quickly. Tell me his name, who did this?'

'His na...*me*...*is*...... ...*E*......' But her words faded to nothing.

The darkness spun around him, whooshing and draining away. Pain shot back into his body as he crashed to a wooden floor.

Panting, he opened his eyes. Rose and Mystic Mogg looked down on him.

'Are you okay?' said Rose. Her backpack's claw reached out and helped him back up.

Eric patted himself down. 'Yeah, I'm fine. I spoke to the dead.'

Rose's eyes widened. 'What did they say?'

The pit of Eric's stomach rumbled at the thought of becoming trapped in eternity with a bunch of self-important adventurers. 'They can't go to the afterlife until we stop the curse.'

'Blimey,' said Rose. 'No pressure then.'

Suddenly, the curtains at the back of the shack flung aside. A pale woman appeared, her razor-sharp teeth glinting in the candlelight. Her robe was black as night, matching her hair that appeared tussled from sleep.

'Hello, Eric,' she said with a grin. 'Long time no see.'

18

Skwee, the goblin, quickened his step to keep up with Edwardius as they marched down the darkened passageway. They followed beside a giant pipe that oozed a brown-green slime between its seams, reminding Skwee of his brood-mother's home-cooked Swamp Soup. He resisted the urge to take a nibble and see how it tasted. The pipe was about twice Edwardius' height and he was already tall for a human. If he still counted as human, that was. Edwardius' face was white and melted, his hair thin and corpse-like. The way he moved was lumbering and pained. But what separated him most from other humans was his aroma. He reeked of death—and also lavender soap due to Skwee's helpfully planned skincare regime.

Skwee tugged at his new robes as they flapped along. He had recently suggested they employ a designer to match all the minions' outfits, a classic way to boost morale and solidify the brand. Edwardius had opted for a traditional black with a splash of acid green for the accent. Skwee also advised that the uniforms should be loose-fitting so that anyone could wear almost any size. For example, even if you were a little too short to be a trooper, you would still look the part. In addition, it meant that if one minion died, their replacement could wear their exact outfit, and they'd save on overheads. This sometimes also meant that any odd wayward nemesis could easily infiltrate the evil lair, incapacitate a minion and take their clothes. But that only happened once a month or so, whereas minions died on a daily basis.

In addition, all minions had been branded with a matching tattoo, which Skwee regretted suggesting almost immediately. He hadn't really thought about it, and then he'd been forced to get one too. The markings of a snake wrapped around a potion were still beetroot red on his arm and stung wherever he moved. All the best dark armies had matching tattoos. It meant that they could easily identify one another out in the wild. Also, brand awareness. It turned out that brand awareness was very important.

Edwardius stopped beside a doorway cut into the rock face, and the rasping of his rusted armour stopped with him.

Skwee looked up at his new master with anticipation. There was a speech incoming, he could feel it. There was a gentle plop as a drip fell from the ceiling and landed in the glass of water Skwee had been holding for the past week.

'I appreciate all your hard work, Skwee,' said Edwardius. Your advice has been most helpful. Thanks to you, I am becoming a true evil overlord.' His voice was gravelly and harsh, making him sound menacing even when being nice—and he was almost always being nice. Which, of course, didn't bode well for his chances of becoming an evil overlord.

'You're welcome,' said Skwee with a polite bow.

'What do you think of the eyeliner? Too much?'

'No, it looks great.'

'And the goatee?'

'All the best evil overlords have a goatee. You can't go wrong with a goatee.'

Edwardius nodded. 'What would I do without you, Skwee?'

Skwee looked down and scuffed the dirt with his bare feet. He wasn't used to this kind of praise. Or any praise, for that matter. It wasn't as if he had much of a choice. Skwee had repeatedly asked to return home to Eric, but all had been rebuffed with veiled threats and emotional blackmail. Skwee wasn't even entirely sure where he was. He hadn't been allowed to leave Edwardius' lair, and there didn't appear to be any windows. That meant they were either very high up or very low down.

'To reward you for your loyal service,' said Edwardius. 'I would like to show you something.'

Edwardius pushed open the doorway and led them inside.

'Behold, my evil masterplan!' he announced, gesturing into the giant room.

He must have meant the massive vat in the middle. However, Skwee wasn't sure what kind of plan that could be. The copper tank glowed green, with hundreds of pipes snaking out and across the walls. It reminded him of some metallic Western contraption Rose might have made. Goblins hurried to and fro—in matching uniforms, of course—carrying vials, clipboards and tools. They splashed across puddles on the cavern floor.

'My Doom Device,' said Edwardius proudly. 'Do you like it? This is what creates my army.'

Skwee scratched his head. Vats of goo didn't make armies. Gold made armies. Or goblins being told what to do.

'Did you know, Skwee, when *the witch* killed me and my darling Felina, I only managed to survive by landing in a giant vat of Elixir? The same Elixir that The Dark Master had a monopoly over, which, since his death, is no longer produced?'

Skwee nodded. His past master, The Dark Master, had sold Elixir to every adventurer across the land, allowing them to heal endlessly. It was where he'd made most of his money.

'Well,' Edwardius continued. 'This is that very same vat. Although it can no longer produce Elixir, it can create something else. My very own concoction. Not one that brings *life*, but instead, *death*. I call it *The Elixir of Death*.'

That was an excellent name, Skwee had to admit it.

'This concoction is what keeps me alive,' Edwardius continued. 'It keeps me from rotting away. It hasn't been easy. I have had to research the ways of the necromancers and learn about their dark arts. Now I have discovered how to harness death itself so that the world can live like me, half dead, half alive.'

He cackled.

'Oh, uh,' stammered Skwee. 'You may want to laugh a little louder. More menacing, you know?'

'Excellent point. How's this?'

Edwardius cackled again. A nearby goblin jumped and dropped its paperwork.

Skwee smiled. 'Perfect! Also, you said you are... sort of... half-dead? It's probably a good idea to claim you're invincible. Even when you're not. It sort of shows you're strong. Then your minions won't question you.'

'Yes, another good point. Thank you, Skwee.' Edwardius cleared his throat. 'Where was I? Ah yes. Any adventurer who drinks *The Elixir of Death* can now turn undead under my control, for it is imbued with stale elixir as well as mine and Felina's blood. Once they are bitten by one of my zombies and infected with the curse, they can no longer be resurrected. Instead, they rise as one of my minions. An army of adventures to do my bidding. These zombies are faster, stronger and fully equipped!'

He cackled loudly again. Skwee gave him a thumbs up.

'No single adventurer is strong enough to defeat The *great* Xenixala,' Edwardius spat at the name and did air quotes around the word great. 'But perhaps *ten thousand* would do it. All at once. Poetic, no?'

'But...' Skwee interjected. 'How do you make the adventurers drink the Elixir?'

'An excellent question, Skwee. For I am pumping *The Elixir of Death* into the water supply. Everyone will eventually drink my cursed water, and when they do, no adventurer will be safe.'

Skwee looked down at the glass of water in his hand. 'But... adventurers don't really drink much water. All they have is beer, wine, potions... and things like that.'

Edwardius smiled wickedly. 'How do you think they *make* beer or wine? Why, with water, of course! The same water that I feed to the breweries.'

Skwee was impressed. It was a clever plan—as if Edwardius had thought of everything. He wasn't really sure what he could help with.

'Now that you finally know my operation,' said Edwardius. 'I have some questions for you. Firstly, do you think I should create a backup vat? I'm concerned that if this one fails, I'll be doomed.'

Skwee shook his head and said sagely, 'No, the training said an evil death machine should never have a backup. It saves on resources.' The training spent a considerable amount of time explaining how to save money. He wondered if they did this so you could spend more money on training courses and magic mirrors. 'Also, it should have a tiny weak point in case you want to disable it, should it fall into the wrong hands.'

'Very good! I will have a weak spot added immediately. I think the topmost valve should do it. Anything else?'

'Oh, and the training also says there should be a self-destruct mechanism, which should be on a long timer and have a big red "OFF" button. Again, in case of emergencies.'

'Consider it done. Anything else?'

'Yes... um... one last thing. I discovered that a bi-monthly evil overlord meeting is coming next week. Are you interested?'

'Is that twice a month, or every two weeks?'

'Oh, uh, I'm not sure, let me check.'

'Please do, as I'm *very* interested...'

19

Major Soothsayer Xenixala of Xendor, Crusher of The Critters, Slayer of Centaurs and writer of countless complaint letters to any shop with 'Ye' in the name, thought: 'hiss' and transformed back into a vampire from a bat. She landed in Porkhaven's unmistakable Wizard's District. The pavements were as misshapen as the mass of wizard's towers that littered the rooftops. The glow of green and pink emanated from places it shouldn't. She shook her foot, flicking off the stale water. It glimmered with the sheen of magic from decades of discarded potions.

She sniffed the air. The street smelled like a rancid blanket. A pack of dogs had been there a few hours ago. For some reason, the scent of canines had become almost unbearable since she had turned. A werewolf passed her a few days prior, and she'd nearly fainted. Holding back the bile in her throat, she continued down the street, and soon found what she was looking for.

The shack resembled every other mystic's shack she had ever seen. Wonky beams held it together, covered by a low, thatched roof that was lumpy with moss.

It had been many years since she had seen Professor Mogg, who had taught her Black Magic in Porkwarts School For-Witches-But-Not-Wizards. That was over a hundred years ago.

How time flew by.

Xenixala knocked on the door, which felt clammy with dampness and rot. She pushed it open without waiting for a response.

Professor Mogg sat in the middle of the shack, wrapped in rags and staring at a crystal ball. The glow illuminated her warty, wrinkled face.

'Xenixala, I knew it was you,' she said without looking up. 'It has been some time.'

The shack was a complete mess of oddities, bones, and poorly made earthenware. She could taste the magic of each one.

Xenixala ran a finger along a shelf and inspected the thick layer of dust on her digit. 'What happened to all the shrunken heads?'

'I knew you would say that,' said Professor Mogg. 'I had too many complaints.'

Xenixala tutted. 'Do you know why I'm here?'

'Of course,' Professor Mogg took her hands off the crystal ball, which went dark. 'You wish to break the vampire's curse.'

'Your ball doesn't leave you with many surprises, does it?'

'Lucky guess.' Professor Mogg smirked, giving Xenixala a pang of insecurity. It was almost as if she had been transported back to the classroom. 'You've got pointy teeth and a face that wants to speak to the manager for a refund. I suppose you got yourself turned and discovered the curse wasn't what you expected?'

'Maybe.'

'And you came here to find a cure.'

Xenixala huffed. Was it really that obvious? 'Perhaps.'

Professor Mogg smiled. 'You haven't changed a bit.' She gestured to the table and chairs in the middle of the room. 'Come, take a seat.'

Xenixala sat at the table, shifting uncomfortably in the chair, which wobbled as she moved. 'I was told that if I found my soul in The Underworld, I could become human again. But I would have to die to reach it.'

Professor Mogg chuckled. 'Yes, I have heard the same. It is a cruel twist of fate, which cannot be done.'

'Well, I wondered if I might be the exception to that.'

Professor Mogg frowned. 'How so?'

Xenixala leaned forward. 'Do you remember helping me create my familiar?'

Professor Mogg nodded slowly. 'Back when I taught you at Porkwarts? My, that was a long, long time ago. But yes, I recall when we made Wordsworth.'

'And a familiar is part of a witch's soul, right? So it's him who I'm looking for, really. And he also just so happens to be a magical tome.'

'And so…'

'Objects *can* be brought back from The Underworld, just not souls. With the right incantation, I might be able to get him back.'

Professor Mogg rubbed her chin, deep in thought. 'Very good. I may still have the original scrolls we used. We could use them as a kind of ward.'

Xenixala tried to stop herself from wriggling with excitement. 'Exactly.'

'It could work… but it would be risky.' Her expression darkened. 'You may be trapped there for all eternity.'

'I'll take my chances.'

'Very well,' said Professor Mogg gravely. She stood up and went into the other room. Soon she returned with an armful of scrolls and potions, which she put on the table.

Xenixala knew Professor Mogg well enough to know she worked better without distraction, so she sat patiently in the corner and let the professor focus on her magic.

After a few hours of mumbling, potion brewing and cups of herbal tea, Professor Mogg looked Xenixala dead in the eye and said, 'It is ready.'

Professor Mogg produced a glass vial and held it up to the light. It sloshed with a dark liquid.

Xenixala gently took the vial and inspected it. 'This will send me there?'

'It will only take you to the gate that catches lost souls on their way to the afterlife. This is part of The Underworld, so you may find that it feels familiar. Then, you must follow the same path that Wordsworth took. That is all I know.'

'Sounds like a plan.' She drank the potion in one gulp and wiped her mouth. It tasted like linseed mixed with blood.

Professor Mogg nodded. 'Although your mind will travel to The Underworld, your physical form will remain here. I suggest you lie down.'

Xenixala followed Professor Mogg into the back room behind a curtain. It was only just big enough for the single bed, which was ruffled with simple hemp sheets and a straw pillow. She shuddered as she lay down on it, making a mental note to bathe in anti-louse cream once this was all over.

Professor Mogg pressed something metal into Xenixala's palm. 'Oh, and you may need this coin. Don't forget it.'

Xenixala slipped it into her robe pocket. She could spend it later on the cream.

Professor Mogg continued soothingly, 'Now, close your eyes and try to imagine yourself insi...'

The world sucked into itself with a great whoosh.

Her mind span. Her heart raced. Her stomach turned.

Blackness was all around her. She gasped, but nothing entered her lungs. The darkness sparkled and expanded, stretching out before her like the ocean.

She blinked. It *was* an ocean.

There was the sound of water gently lapping against the sand. She could feel the ground beneath her feet again, but when she looked down, nothing was there. Somehow, the darkness pushed against her toes. She looked up to see a great body of black water, almost invisible against the blackness all around her. The waves shimmered as they lolled far into the horizon.

One thing she remembered from her last trip to The Underworld was that mysterious liquids were not to be trusted (nor were any bargains or pacts offered by oddly attractive demons), so she resisted the urge to wade into the dark ocean. Instead, she began to walk along its edge. She decided to go right instead of left, as she somehow felt that's what Wordsworth would have done.

She continued to walk for what felt like hours, which seemed particularly futile as the horizon remained the same empty darkness no matter how far she travelled. She stopped with a huff and sat down. Perhaps this was the end. Had she made a terrible mistake? Was an eternity of darkness all that was left of her existence?

Just as she considered throwing herself into the water out of sheer despair, she heard a faint rhythmic splashing sound. The sound grew louder, and she soon saw where it came from. A cloaked figure in a tiny rowing boat approached her across the water. The figure remained eerily still while the oars moved with a life of their own.

The boat reached the shoreline and stopped. The hooded figure raised its head towards her, but the shadow of its cloak concealed its face.

'Who are *you*?' said Xenixala, cursing herself for sounding patronising.

'They call me "He Who Sails",' he replied, his voice hollow and rasping. 'But that's a bit fancy if you know what I mean. A bit pompous, like. But I didn't come up with it. That's just what they call me. Anyway, who are you?'

'I'm...' she resisted the urge to list some of her many titles. The creature clearly had an issue with them. 'Xenixala.'

'Hello, Xen-i-k... Xeiny... Xe... Sorry, can I just call you Zen?'

'As you wish,' she said, smiling at the thought of adding another name to the list.

'Right, Zen. So what are you doing on my shore? I don't get a lot of folks this far along. There ain't been anyone come this way for a good millennium or so, I'd wager. Most come in the front. Know what I mean? Much easier in the front way. Less rowing, for one thing.'

Xenixala folded her arms. 'You don't even do the rowing.'

He Who Sails scratched the top of his head with a pale, bony finger. 'Well, no. Not strictly speaking. But I steer—and it takes time to get around, you know? Still takes time. Anyway, you didn't answer my question.'

Xenixala didn't know if the truth was the best policy. Underworld minions tended to trick people at every turn in a desperate attempt to steal their souls or wallets.

'I'm looking for a lost object of mine,' she said carefully. 'A talking book, in fact. Would you happen to know how to find it?'

'Hmm... I don't. But I could take you to the fella who does... for a price. I'd have to row you across the far side of The Sea of Souls, you see. That'll cost ya.'

And there it was. There was always a price.

'But I don't have anything. I came here with nothing.'

'Oh really?' said He Who Sails in a coy tone. 'I can smell a coin a mile away. Why do you think I came here so fast?'

Xenixala patted her pockets and felt the thin, hard lump. She pulled out the coin that Professor Mogg had given her.

He Who Sails nodded. 'That'll do! Alright, hop in and we'll get going.'

Xenixala had long since learned that jumping into transportation with strangers rarely ended well. She considered her other options. And considered that there weren't any. Throwing caution to the wind, she clambered into the tiny boat, tossed him the coin—and they pushed off into the darkness.

20

Skwee looked out across the sea of zombies from a balcony high above. The mass of bodies stretched as far as the eye could see, or at least as far as the dim cavern light allowed. Their groans and hisses were deafening, which he'd alleviated by squishing up his earwax to make a seal. At this point, he'd become pretty used to the smell of rotting zombies, but this was almost unbearable. He held his breath and looked up at Edwardius beside him, who beamed, revealing the misshapen cracks on his face.

'Do you think I'm ready?' said Edwardius, straightening his black doublet. 'How do I look? I'm a little nervous.'

Behind them stood the creature Edwardius called Felina. The zombie pixie was kept in chains, but periodically attempted to bite whoever was closest. Edwardius claimed they were once fierce lovers, but Skwee had difficulty believing it. She was just a horrible little corpse.

'Don't worry, master,' said Skwee. 'Being an evil overlord is all about *confidence. Fake-itilyoumakit,* if you want the official term.'

'You think so?'

'I know so! It doesn't matter what you're feeling inside. Show them you're strong and in control. With enough confidence, anyone can be an evil overlord. It's supposed to be that easy.'

Edwardius nodded and straightened his back, surveying the scene from the balcony.

'What a beautiful sight!' Edwardius breathed deeply, somehow enjoying the awful smell. 'A whole army of undead ready to strike —adventurers and peasants alike. Soon, they will bite every person in the land, passing on my curse and turning them undead at my command.'

Skwee felt a knot in his stomach. He quite liked people. Some of them were his friends. If everyone was a zombie, would he have to be a zombie, too? Maybe this was like the tattoo he'd suggested. His arm still stung from the shoddy needlework. He looked down at the glass of water in his hand and sighed. He had to find Eric and give him his water, or they all might end up like the poor people down there. Maybe he was already too late.

Edwardius cleared his throat and stepped towards the balustrade.

'My loyal minions!' he shouted. The zombies went quiet in response. 'Are you ready to bring the world to its knees?!'

Silence.

Edwardius awkwardly shuffled from side to side, then turned to Skwee. 'I'm not sure they can all hear me? They're awfully far away.'

'Um, yes, but...' Skwee whispered. 'Aren't they zombies? I don't think they could reply even if they wanted to?'

Edwardius bashed his palm on his forehead. 'Silly me! I'm controlling them.'

Edwardius turned back to face the crowd and raised his arms. The zombies erupted in rasps of joy.

'Ah, there we are.'

Skwee gave him the thumbs up.

'My minions!' Edwardius continued. 'It is time to take control! To get our... *my* revenge! The world will soon be like my dearest Felina! Huzzah!'

The zombies chanted in unison—with a groan that sounded a little bit like "huzzah".

Skwee wondered why Edwardius bothered doing a speech to zombies when his magic was controlling them. It would be good for his ego, so Skwee didn't say anything. Although his zombies must have had some degree of autonomy. There was no way his mind could handle that many things at once.

'Here are your standing orders. The D-Team will strike first, followed by the C-Team and the B-Team. The A-Team will surround the lair as my personal guard! Do I make myself clear?'

The swathe of zombies wheezed agreeably.

Edwardius turned to Skwee. 'See, I remembered about "the hierarchy of waste". I'm sending the weakest waves first...'

Skwee nodded. 'To save on overheads, good job, master.'

'I've been saving the strongest adventuring zombies until now. The peasant zombies have been doing most of the work across the land thus far. Now we can move to Phase Three and unleash the full force of the horde.'

'Um,' Skwee stammered. 'What is Phase Three again, master?'

'Why, the showdown with my nemesis, of course! With the *witch*.' Edwardius spat on the dirt. 'It's just how you explained—a nemesis can fuel you and make you stronger. My hatred of her has created me and therefore all this.' He gestured to the zombies far below. 'And I have you to thank, too, of course. But now it is time for the greatest showdown the world has ever seen.' He turned to Felina behind them, who rattled in her chains. 'And my dearest Felina, we will have our sweet, sweet revenge. *Xenixala* will pay dearly for what she did to us.'

Skwee looked down sheepishly. 'Master... now that everything is almost over... do you think you could let me... go home?'

Edwardius tutted. 'Leave now! But we're only just beginning! What would I do without you?' He patted Skwee on the head, then wiped his hand on his sleeve. 'No, I'm sorry, Skwee, but we have so much work to do. You can go home once we are done.'

'Okay, master.'

'Excellent. We are moving to Phase Three because my spies have seen *Xenixala* enter the city. For some reason, I have been unable to sense her soul until now... But she has finally been spotted. So now it is time to strike before I lose her again.'

'Okay, master.'

'And Skwee, be a dear and bring me my tea, would you?'

'Okay, master.'

Skwee padded away. He continued down the corridors of the evil lair until he reached the kitchens. But he hesitated at the door.

What was he thinking? This had gone on long enough.

He had to take control.

He should take his own advice. He needed to be confident, take action. This was his only chance.

But could he disobey a master? Every fibre of his being resisted. Conformity was safe. Conformity was comfortable.

But this conformity was going to turn the world into smelly zombies. Everyone he had ever known would be gone. He clenched Eric's glass of water tightly. Edwardius wasn't his master, not really. *Eric* was his master. That meant he could disobey Edwardius, and technically, it would be okay.

Content with his decision, he turned and scurried down a side path.

In the weeks he'd been trapped there, he'd become pretty familiar with the patterns of the warrens of the evil lair. A goblin's intuition was good at tunnels. They made *sense* somehow, in a way that streets and straight lines didn't. He knew there would be a way out if he followed his nose. There was fresh air coming from one direction. It was unmistakable.

He sniffed the air and took a right.

Closer.

There was a metal grate on the wall. The air coming through it made his arm hair flutter. There had to be a way out. He pulled at the metal bars; luckily, they fell away without too much resistance.

The tunnel it led to was round and low, only just tall enough for him to stand in. Water trickled at his feet, and he followed it towards the light shining at the end.

The light grew and grew. He could almost taste his freedom.

He reached it to discover a small pond at the bottom of a shaft. The light cascaded from high above. A chain hung all the way, ending deep in the water.

Skwee didn't hesitate. He jumped onto the chain and climbed, which was particularly tricky while balancing a glass of water clenched between his teeth.

He clambered out of the hole and landed in a puddle of mud. He winced at the light of the sky he hadn't seen in weeks. There was a fresh, memorable aroma.

Someone kicked him.

'Wait your turn,' said the figure with a bucket. 'Get to the back of the line. There's a queue.'

Skwee looked up. He was by a well.

An oddly familiar well.

In fact, it was the very same well where he'd met Catch, which had got him kidnapped in the first place. He hadn't actually gone very far at all. In a way, it was quite a relief.

Skwee apologised to the disgruntled human and jumped to his feet. He darted through the muddied streets of Porkhaven towards the Beast Be Gone store, pushing aside the various denizens.

He needed to warn Eric.

And also give him his glass of water.

21

Master Mage Xenixala of Xendor, Myth of The Knife, Known to He Who Sails as "Zen" and the human to have officially killed more goblins than all other things put together, held her hand over the side of the rowing boat, hovering it above the dark water.

'I wouldn't do that if I were you,' said He Who Sails. 'That water's pretty 'orrible. Full of evil and dread and things like that. Nasty stuff that'll suck you under and won't let go. Not that it is water *as such*... I like to think of it as soup for demons.'

Xenixala recoiled her hand back into the confines of the boat. She hunched her knees up, but they still bashed into the legs of the creature-or-person sitting across from her. The vessel lolled while they rowed along, the oars moving with a mind of their own.

She shifted on the wooden plank. The whole thing was deeply uncomfortable. He could at least have some pillows or something.

'This demon soup,' she said, her interest piqued by the mention of evil. 'You call it The Sea Of Souls?'

'Yeah,' said He Who Sails. He stared at her through the darkness of his hood. Something told Xenixala that she didn't need to see what was hidden under there. 'Soul soup. But for demons, you know?' He turned to survey the emptiness of the black ocean all around them, blanketed by a sky of nothingness. 'Feels like home, doesn't it? Glorious.' He breathed deeply, wafting his pallid hands towards where his face ought to be. 'Smell that? That's fresh soul, that is. Nothing beats it.'

Xenixala grimaced. 'So what *are* you, exactly?'

'I'm He Who Sails, I told ya.'

'I know your *name*. But what are you doing here? Is this some kind of job?'

'Ha!' He Who Sails chortled. 'If it were a job, I'd get paid! Nah, I don't get much say in the matter. It's just who I am. I sail people. Without me, no one gets across the Sea Of Souls.'

'So you're a glorified ferryman.'

'If you like, yeah.'

'And you take people to the afterlife?'

'Sometimes, but most souls go straight there. I'm here to pick up the stragglers.' He sniffed stiffly. 'There's been an awful lot of those around lately. Awful lot. A bit too cursed for my liking, though. Won't be able to get them in the boat. Which is a shame, really. They sure do make an awful mess down here. I tend to avoid those shores. Not that I've been on them, mind you.'

Too cursed to sail a cursed boat across a sea of demons sounded about as cursed as could be. 'You don't leave your boat?'

'Not sure I can, to be honest. I've never even used my legs. They seem a bit, what's the word, vestige? Vur-stitch... *verstigial*. Yeah. Vestigial. If you know what I mean. I don't need 'em. They look the part, though, I suppose.' He stretched out his feet, which poked from the bottom of his black robe. He wiggled his toes, showing off his gnarled yellow toenails.

Xenixala tried not to retch. 'If this *isn't* a job, and you never leave this boat, what will you do with that coin I gave you?'

'I've gotta pay for upkeep, don't I?' He tapped the vessel's side, which made a sad, hollow *thunk*. 'Hard to find good wood down here, let me tell you. See any trees? Then there's the taxes and the maritime licence and all that. Adds up.'

It didn't surprise her that The Underworld had a hellish bureaucracy. She nodded. 'So where are you taking me, and how far is it?'

'Well, you said you're looking for a lost book, right? I reckon you'll wanna speak to The Librarian. He keeps tabs on all things down here. Very organised chap. You have to be, to be a librarian. That's kinda their whole thing. He'd probably know where a book would end up.'

'If you say so.'

He Who Sails spent the rest of their journey rabbiting on about all hundred different currents in The Sea of Souls and which oar stroke worked best in each of them. She ignored him and instead focussed on not falling asleep, fearing that in The Underworld, she wouldn't be able to wake up.

After what felt like an eternity, they arrived at a shore that seemed more solid than the one she'd departed from. In fact, it had stone edging and a neat path leading off into a black haze.

'Here you are,' said He Who Sails triumphantly. 'The Under Library. Just follow that path there.'

Xenixala clambered out of the boat and onto the stone. It felt cool and reassuring beneath her feet. 'I appreciate it,' she said.

'I'll see you around Zen, but not *too* soon, if you know what I mean. I hope you find what you're looking for.'

'Me too.'

The boat oars began moving again—and He Who Sails returned to the sea.

Xenixala turned and walked down the path, glad that the endless rabbiting of the ferryman had ceased.

Shortly, a great stone structure appeared, stretching into the darkness. The facade was adorned with thousands of statues in little alcoves, each staring vacantly into the sheer emptiness beyond. The towering door was ajar, emitting a glowing light towards her. She winced. Light felt somehow *wrong*. She shielded her eyes and went inside.

She stopped in disbelief.

Countless books sat on countless shelves, going on up into infinity. The amber glow of candles flickered on every shelf, creating a surprisingly charming effect—almost as if a swarm of glow bugs had infested the library.

She breathed in deep, relishing the scent of dusty books and oak. She'd always enjoyed a good library, but this was the library to top them all. It looked like it had more books than had ever been written.

Someone cleared their throat. She looked down to see a man standing before her. His faded white robes fell loosely over his hunched back. He had a bundle of scrolls in his arms. 'Can I help you, young lady?' he whispered.

Xenixala tried to conceal her enjoyment at being called a young lady when she was well over a hundred years old. 'Yes... I'm looking for The Librarian.'

'Ah,' said the man, 'Then you have found him. But please lower your voice.'

'Oh, sorry,' she whispered back.

'So what can I do for you? I assume you want a book?'

'Naturally. Quite a specific book, in fact. One that belongs to me. He's called...'

'Wordsworth?' The Librarian cut in.

'Yes! How did you...?'

The Librarian sighed. 'He's been talking about you nonstop. The Great Xenixala is it? I can barely shut him up.'

That sounded like Wordsworth, alright. 'So you found him?'

'In a sense. He ended up here long ago, and he's been driving me potty since the moment he arrived. This is a *library*. I've put him in charge of filing the new scriptures to keep him busy. And quiet.'

'I'll be happy to take him off your hands.'

The Librarian nodded. 'Let me take you to him.'

He led her to a door hidden between the bookshelves. It squeaked open, and they ducked to pass through it.

The room was full of book piles, unravelled scrolls and stacks of paper.

'Sorry about the mess,' said the Librarian sheepishly.

A pile trembled, and its books tumbled aside. Wordsworth, the spellbook popped up between them, shaking off the loose pages.

'Xeni!' Wordsworth exclaimed.

The Librarian tutted.

'*Xeni*!' Wordsworth whispered and flapped to the floor. His pages riffled with excitement.

'Wordsworth!' Xenixala whispered back. She almost scooped him up in her arms but thought it would be too soppy. There was a tingle of warmth in her chest. For a split second, she felt alive again. Then, the feeling melted away, and the hollowness washed back over her. 'How'd you end up here?'

Wordsworth curved his spine in a shrug. 'I'm not completely sure. Once you'd been bitten, I woke up floating in a black sea and eventually washed up on a kind of shore. Then, this fellow found me and took me in. I've been working for him ever since.'

'Making a mess, more like,' huffed the Librarian. 'He doesn't understand my system *at all*.'

'You need a better system,' said Wordsworth. 'It makes no sense. You can't organise a library in five dimensions without creating a booktorial paradox…'

The Librarian sighed and turned to Xenixala. 'You see what I've been dealing with?'

'Don't worry,' said Xenixala, 'I'll take him with me now.'

'Were it that simple,' said the Librarian. 'I've been researching vampire curses and familiar soul bonding. He cannot leave The Underworld with you. He needs to be resurrected. And for one as powerful as the vampire's curse, only the most experienced necromancer can do it.'

Xenixala rubbed her temples. This whole adventure had descended into a series of fetch quests. 'How will they know what to do?'

The Librarian produced a scrap of paper from his sleeve. 'Take this incantation. A mighty necromancer can use it to reunite your body and soul.' He knelt and ripped a corner from one of Wordsworth's pages.

'*Ow*!' Wordsworth yelped.

The Librarian stood up. 'Normally, for a human soul, you would extract a lock of hair or some-such. But this will have to do.' He handed Xenixala the tiny scrap of Wordsworth. 'That will bind the spell back here to The Underworld, so don't lose it.'

She took both pieces of paper and slipped them into her pocket. 'I won't. Now, how do I get back to the real world?'

'Oh, that's easy,' said The Librarian. 'You just say: "I wish I were back home."'

'Really? Just, "I wish I were back home…?"'

Darkness.

Xenixala sat up, gasping for air.

The room whirled.

Her mouth felt dryer than a troll's toenail.

She was back in Professor Mogg's hut. That was apparent from the stink of incense and the mouldy wood.

She got up from the bed, throwing back the musky sheet. She steadied herself on the wall and breathed deeply.

Muffled voices were coming from next door.

Familiar voices.

She smiled, pulling back the curtain and stepping into the light.

'Hello, Eric,' she said with a grin. 'Long time no see.'

22

Eric couldn't believe his eyes. After all this time. It was her. Xenixala.

He didn't know why, but his stomach felt like it had turned upside down. Mystic Mogg's shack spun around him. Was this another vision? Was he still in The Underworld? No, the shack's stench of incense was too alive, not to mention the eclectic trinkets, which looked too corporeal.

'Good to... see you too,' he stammered. His hand took it upon itself to discreetly tidy his hair. He hadn't seen Xenixala since they'd toppled the adventuring craze the year before. She'd killed The Dark Master, saved them all, and then disappeared without a thank-you-or-goodbye. They'd only spent about a day together, but somehow, it seemed he'd known her forever.

'Eric and his merry band of not-adventurers,' said Xenixala as she looked Rose up and down. Her way of speaking made everything sound like an insult. 'What are *you* doing here?'

'I could ask you the same question,' said Eric, folding his arms.

Mystic Mogg's gaze flitted between them. A grin appeared on her face like an additional wrinkle. 'I see you two have met. I thought I sensed something when you both arrived. Surely the stars have...'

'A coincidence, nothing more,' Xenixala cut in, much to Eric's relief.

Rose's eyes narrowed at Xenixala, her whole body poised to strike. 'Your teeth...' Rose's voice wavered. 'You're a vampire now, aren't you?'

Xenixala huffed. 'Not that it's any of your business, but yes.'

Eric could smell the curse on her but hadn't wanted to bring it up. Vampires were touchy creatures at the best of times. Combine that with a narcissistic witch, and you have a recipe for pure chaos. They'd be lucky to see daylight again if they made the wrong move. He wondered if she could smell his curse on him, too. She probably didn't need to. He was dripping with sweat, and every time he moved, he felt like he was about to topple over.

'And how's that going for you?' said Eric, mopping his brow.

'Wonderfully. Thank you very much. I've never been better.'

'She's here for a cure,' said Mystic Mogg matter-of-factly.

Xenixala looked like she was about to boil. Her cheeks would have likely turned red had she not afflicted herself with a white-skinned curse. Eric regarded the glares shared between Mystic Mogg and Xenixala. They must have had a history. And Xenixala appeared to have a begrudging respect for the mystic. Otherwise, he was sure the mystic's head would have rolled for the comment.

Xenixala turned back to Eric and pulled her lips into an acidic smile. 'Yes, if you must know. I was looking for a cure. The vampire's curse has stripped me of my soul and, therefore, Wordsworth. It would be cruel to leave him trapped in The Underworld, so I was trying to get him back.'

'I'm sorry to hear that.' Eric had become strangely fond of the chatty book. You could talk to him without fear of becoming a toad. Reversing a vampire's curse was impossible, so Wordsworth would be long gone. Whatever she was attempting was futile.

'Indeed,' said Xenixala, 'Anyway, what are you two doing here? Shooing away some kind of poltergeist who keeps moving a lord's chamber pot?'

'*Actually*,' said Eric through gritted teeth. I'm dealing with this zombie problem—a problem you would have noticed if you weren't too busy hiding in the shadows.'

'Lucky for you, I have noticed.' Xenixala suddenly sounded oddly pleasant. 'These zombies are quite the irksome rabble. Such disgusting creatures. I approve. And how do you plan on doing that?'

'We have to find the necromancer who created the curse,' said Eric. 'I've just been to The Underworld myself to ask the souls of those afflicted. A pixie said her beloved is behind the whole thing.'

Xenixala's eyes narrowed. 'Did she happen to be called... Felina?'

Somehow, Eric wasn't surprised. Xenixala had wrapped herself up in just about everything. Every lord spoke as if she were the boogey man. Every township had some kind of mess he'd needed to clean up after her. It had provided Beast Be Gone with a lot of work, so he was thankful for that, at least. 'A friend of yours, was she?'

Xenixala looked like she'd seen a ghost. When, in fact, she'd only heard about one. 'Not a friend... more a *rival*. We adventured together until... I got both her and her beloved killed.'

Eric nodded. Death was the inevitable conclusion to Xenixala's escapades. 'She told me her beloved used her blood to make the curse. Who are they, anyway?'

Xenixala smiled. 'Felina was a pointy, perfect pixie, and her so-called "beloved" Edwardius was a poncy, puritanical paladin.' Every "p" popped with distaste. 'They were in my way, so I had to deal with them. Right before I dealt with The Dark Master for you, in fact.'

'I see. So we're looking for a paladin called Edwardius. That can't be too hard.'

Xenixala stepped towards him, smiling. She leaned on the table in an attempt to seem nonchalant. 'Eric... it sounds like you might... need some help. As I know Edwardius personally, perhaps I could be of assistance?'

There was something she wasn't telling them. Xenixala's connection to Felina and Edwardius was probably messy and dangerous. However, he didn't have many other options. He'd have to keep plenty of garlic in his back pocket, just in case.

Rose shook her head. 'You'll just abandon us like you did last time!'

Xenixala made a face of false concern. 'I wouldn't dream of it.'

Eric grunted. 'You're welcome to tag along if you promise to do as I ask *and* not abandon us when it suits you.'

'Of course,' said Xenixala.

'Alright then, let's get back to the shop and make a plan.'

'Deal.'

'Goodbye, you three,' said Mystic Mogg as they left the shack. 'Don't do anything I wouldn't do.'

They wandered out into the darkened streets of Porkhaven. The moon shone, sending a silver glow across the cobblestones and wonky rooftops. Eric breathed in the air. Despite the hint of rank meat, it smelled like home.

He led them down Gullbottom Alley, which was the opposite of the scenic route. Although it would shave a few minutes off their walk to the Beast Be Gone shop. Alleys had foolishly got a bad reputation in Porkhaven. People assumed they were more dangerous because they were darker and had fewer escape paths. However, the bandits and thieves had long since learned that if they hid in an alley, they could wait weeks without seeing another soul. It was far more efficient to assault people on the main routes. Considering how many enchanted weapons, magic spells and god-like denizens there were, a well-lit and open street gave the thief the same means of escape as their victims.

Xenixala yawned. 'I could have flown there by now.'

'What's stopping you?' Eric tucked his overalls in a little bit tighter to seal from the chill.

'If I flew off, it would only annoy you,' said Xenixala. 'And I want to help. I'm quite keen to improve my reputation, you see. Saving the land from a plague of zombies should put me back into people's good books.'

'Oh,' said Eric, taken aback. Maybe turning into a vampire had somehow softened her up.

They exited the alley onto the lower end of Pickleburrow High Street. Glinting shops advertised their wares behind sheets of expensive glass—naturally all enchanted and shatter-proof.

A large crowd blocked their path. Was there an event going on? Maybe some posh art show where paint splashes made people say: "*My eight-year-old could have done that.*"

Oh no.

The crowd groaned and turned towards them. Their open wounds dripped and oozed, which would have incapacitated even the hardiest of dwarves. In fact, some of them *were* dwarves. Even elves, goblins and halflings joined the ranks of the dead. Most brandished weapons and were clad in armour. Some even wielded their own severed limbs as crude clubs.

'Urm, Eric...' Rose stammered.

Eric whipped the crossbow from his back. 'Yes, I see them.'

More moans came from behind.

Another wall of zombies.

Eric swung around, looking for a way out. Slowly, hundreds of corpses closed in on them.

They were trapped.

Xenixala rolled her eyes. 'They're really not so bad.'

'That's easy for you to say,' Eric hissed. 'You're a vampire. The undead don't go for their own. There's nothing to eat.'

'I thought they just knew their place,' said Xenixala, scratching her chin.

'These aren't your normal zombies,' said Eric. 'These are adventurers... and even minions, it seems. They might have changed their minds about leaving you alone.'

'I see,' said Xenixala, straightening her back and cracking her knuckles. 'Well, let's get killing then, shall we?'

Rose muttered something about them already being dead, then pulled the lever on her backpack. The bronze arm glinted in the moonlight as the claw spun into action. She nodded.

The zombies charged.

They moved faster than anything he'd ever seen. His body tensed and his leg throbbed. He gritted his teeth and pulled the trigger.

The crossbow bolt pierced through the skull of a bard, lopping its head clean off. A lyre clattered to the floor.

Rose leapt aside as two knights clashed into one another, their plate mail clanging as they fell. Her claw smashed both of their heads in rapid succession.

Eric shot another bolt and looked back at Xenixala. 'Aim for the...'

'For the head,' said Xenixala, who had yet to move. 'Yeah, I know.'

She sighed, then dashed.

She moved even faster than the undead. Her hands lashed out like claws, tearing off limbs and heads. Green-grey blood rained down around her as she dove into the horde. She jumped into the air, spinning gracefully, her face beaming with delight.

Eric froze. It was a sight to behold. She made it look effortless.

She landed in the crowd. It exploded, sending blobs of flesh and guts in all directions.

Eric wiped his face and drew his dagger.

A pixie ran at him, thrashing half an arm, baring its teeth.

Eric swiped left and right, but the zombie didn't even flinch as the blade sliced its belly and throat. Eric took a step back, then stabbed forward into its eye. The blade went straight through the soft, rotten meat. The zombie crumpled to the ground.

But then there were six more on him.

He needed something else. There were too many.

Rose yelped as a skull-exposed barbarian grabbed her by the throat. Her robotic arm span and struck it again and again until its head was nothing but mush. Rose tumbled away, the arm snapping down to catch her fall.

Eric whipped out his Bag of Clutching and delved deep.

The scroll appeared in his hand.

'Undeadiues Boggofferus, Expleahatus!' He read the scroll's incantation just as the zombies reached him.

The scroll exploded with light.

Pain rushed through his body. A resounding boom knocked the creatures back.

All the zombies tumbled to the floor. They writhed on the ground, dazed. But alive.

Curious.

A scroll of Turn-Dead-Level-Seven obliterated almost any basic undead at this close range. These were much stronger zombies than he thought possible. The scrolls weren't cheap, either.

His head pounded. He was halfway to being undead himself, as the curse was in him too. He could have kicked himself for being so stupid. The scroll was a terrible idea. He almost killed them all. Xenixala would be fine, though. Vampires were far too powerful for scrolls.

Xenixala stared at him across the groaning bodies that struggled to stand back up. 'You could have warned me!' she called out. 'That's given me a headache.'

'Quick,' said Eric. 'We need to kill them while they're down.'

'You don't have to tell me twice,' said Xenixala as she stomped on a head with a squelch.

23

Skwee awoke as the door burst open. Rose, Eric and *that-evil-witch* stumbled into the shop, all panting and covered in dark slime. They smelled a lot better than usual—not unlike the tail end of the meat market after a sunny day. Usually, they reeked of horrible flowery things that humans were fond of rubbing themselves with.

Eric slammed the door behind them and bolted it.

Skwee got up from his nest in the corner and rubbed his eyes. He'd arrived at the Beast Be Gone shop and found it deserted, aside from Larry, who didn't really count because he was, quite literally, part of the furniture.

Skwee had whiled the hours away by tidying up and dusting—as the housekeeping had been sorely neglected in his absence. Doing his jobs had filled him with such a sense of belonging and comfort that he'd felt uncontrollably sleepy. So he'd curled up in the corner and caught some much-needed rest.

'Master!' he exclaimed. 'You're back!' He wanted to hug Eric but thought it wouldn't be his place. So, instead, he bowed.

'Only just,' said Eric, plopping himself behind his desk. He looked paler than usual, with deep, sullen eyes. His whole body shook as he reached for the whisky in his drawer. 'Skwee, where did you go? I was about to put up posters with your face on them.'

Skwee held up the glass of water. It had turned a delicious murky grey after all of his careful carrying. 'I went to get you this, but I... got sidetracked.'

Eric looked at his bottle, then back at the water. 'I think I'll stick to the whisky for now. Thank you, Skwee.' He took the glass of water and placed it gingerly on the desk. Skwee assumed he wanted to save it as a treat for later.

The horrible sorceress they called Xenixala surveyed their beautiful shop and scowled. 'Couldn't you afford some kind of renovation? Shouldn't business be booming after the adventurers returned to their regular jobs and left you to mop up?'

'Business is fine,' Rose huffed. 'We happen to love it here. It has a rustic charm.'

Xenixala snorted. 'For a farm shop, perhaps.'

Skwee had to agree. The shop's messy charm, with its shelves of trinkets and piles of paperwork, somehow felt right. Putting fancy panelling over the whitewashed walls would be like turning an inn into a bank. Sure, it would look nice, but nobody would be happy there anymore.

'If you don't like it...' Eric took a swig of whisky straight from the bottle and winced. 'Then you're welcome to leave. We can fight Edwardius on our own.'

'You couldn't handle all those zombies without me,' said Xenixala. 'The streets are too infested. It's a walking graveyard out there.'

Skwee gulped. Edwardius had executed his plan just as he'd promised. It wouldn't be long before the whole city was dead undead. Curiously, they'd somehow learned all about Edwardius for themselves.

'Well, I'm not going anywhere anytime soon,' said Eric. 'I can barely sit up.' Eric took a piece of jerky meat from his bag and tossed it at the lamp in the corner. The lamp twisted and reshaped into a wooden chest. The chest opened, revealing a thick tongue that licked out and snapped the jerky from the air.

'Thanks, Eric,' said Larry, the mimic. 'I was starving! It's been jolly lonely in here. Where have you all been?'

'That's a good question,' said Eric. He coughed, then wiped his mouth and leaned back in his chair. 'Skwee, where *have* you been exactly? Sidetracked where?'

'Oh, me?' Skwee stammered. 'Why, I...'

This was his moment. All eyes were on him.

He clenched his fists and stood up straight. He wasn't a minion anymore. He had to take control, to be strong. He was a goblin with his own personality with thoughts and feelings and power.

He was Skwee.

'I...' he continued. 'I went out and infiltrated Edwardius's lair.'

Stunned silence.

The humans' mouths hung open like fish about to be fed in a pond.

'How did you...' said Rose, her brow furrowed. 'We only just...'

Skwee cleared his throat. 'It was an intuition I had. The adventurer zombies were coming from somewhere. So... I did some investigating and found his secret base in Porkhaven. They thought I was just another minion. So I walked in, no questions asked.'

Skwee didn't think he'd ever said something that wasn't true before. What did the humans call it? Lying. It felt strange. His mind knew what he said was false, but when he spoke the words, it became true. Is this how humans took over the world so easily?

'That's... extraordinary, Skwee,' said Eric. 'I'm incredibly impressed. Great job.'

Skwee beamed.

This was the best day of his life. However, a lot of that had to do with the fantastic nap.

Eric mopped his brow with a handkerchief and winced. 'A ghost pixie called Felina told us about this Edwardius. She said he's made a zombie curse out of her blood that can turn even adventurers into zombies. She also said he's hiding somewhere in Porkhaven. Do you think you could lead us there?'

'I could!' said Skwee. 'He's in the sewers. You can go down the local well and through the tunnels. Somehow...' He scratched his chin. 'Although I'm not too sure about which tunnels *exactly*... I kinda just followed my nose. I might be able to smell my way back.'

'This seems a little too convenient,' said Xenixala, eyeing Skwee up and down. 'What if this creature has sided with Edwardius and plans to lead us into a trap? He's a goblin. Goblins famously can't be trusted.'

Eric smiled at Skwee. 'I'd trust Skwee with my life.' He coughed into his handkerchief and frowned at the blood smatters.

Skwee leapt into action. 'You haven't drunk your water, master!' He picked up the half-full-of-cloudy-goodness glass and pushed it into Eric's hands. 'It will make you feel better.'

Eric took it with a weak smile. 'Okay, Skwee. Thank you.' He raised it to his lips.

Something tickled at the back of Skwee's head. Something wasn't right. Something about the water...

'No!' he screamed. He batted the glass away—and it smashed to the floor. 'The water is poisoned!'

'Ha!' Xenixala scoffed. 'I knew the goblin was up to no good.'

'It's not me, master, honest,' said Skwee. 'Edwardius is poisoning the water supply. He said he's using the old Elixir vats to allow adventurers to become zombies— *The Elixir of Death,* he calls it. He has a Doom Device and everything.'

All the humans drew breath.

'Ah...' said Eric. 'We've all already drunk quite a bit of water. Plus, any of the fun drinks that water goes in...' He glanced at the bottle of whisky. 'I think that ship has sailed.'

'So that's how he's doing it,' said Rose, scratching her chin. 'If what Skwee says is true... then Edwardius must be under The Dark Master's Doom Bank! The one we destroyed last year?'

'In fact,' Xenixala cut in. 'That was where I killed Edwardius before. It's classic evil overlord behaviour.'

'Well done, Skwee,' Eric wheezed.

'It was nothing, really,' said Skwee, blushing.

Rose patted Skwee on the back. 'Now we just have to be quick before Eric transforms into a...'

Eric tumbled from his chair.

'Master!' Skwee cried. He tried to catch Eric's fall. But Eric was too heavy, so Skwee let him roll to the floor. 'Is he dead?!'

Rose's backpack whirred as her claw spun to attention. She stepped back, poised to strike. 'Yes and no... I think he's finally turned.'

'Well done setting up the curse with some drama there,' said Xenixala. 'Good job.'

Rose flashed her a cold stare but didn't respond.

Eric groaned.

It was a dark, hissing groan that rattled as it came through his loose lips. His eyes opened, revealing his now lifeless, pale blue irises.

A zombie.

'What do we do, what do we do!?' Skwee shrieked.

Xenixala shook her head. 'Oh dear. Poor Eric. I knew he would get himself turned sooner or later.'

'We can still save him,' said Rose resolutely. 'We just need to stop Edwardius in order to lift the curse.'

Xenixala tutted as Eric struggled to stand up. *'Fine*, I suppose so. Shall we chain him up until then? Goblin, go and fetch us some chains.'

'Actually...' Rose looked at Larry and then back at Eric. 'I have a better idea.'

*   *   *

'Stop wriggling, Larry,' said Rose as she stepped back to admire her creation. 'You might hurt him.'

'Don't worry,' said Larry. 'I'm quite soft inside.'

Skwee knew that Rose was clever, but not *this* clever. Larry, the mimic, had taken the form of a suit of armour. It was the kind of armour you would find in the castle of a lord who thought fashionable and creepy were the same thing. It would have been far too ornate for a real battle, but it didn't have to be. It just had to fit Eric.

Eric's new zombie form fitted snugly inside the living armour.

'Try walking,' said Rose, encouragingly.

Larry moved his legs. They remained perfectly straight, but he was able to amble forward.

'I should do this more often!' said Larry with delight. 'I feel like a real human being.'

Eric hissed from inside the visor.

Eric's face was only just visible through the slits in the front, his twisted face gnawing and biting helplessly.

'I think I prefer him like this,' said Xenixala. 'His grunts are an improvement.'

'Be nice,' said Rose. 'He might still be able to hear you.'

'I hope he can,' said Xenixala as she pushed Larry. He tottered back and clanked into the wall. 'Crude, but effective, I suppose.'

Rose knelt, bringing her to eye level with Skwee. 'Skwee, we need you to take us to the necromancer's lair. Are you sure you remember the way in?'

'Yes,' Skwee nodded. 'We can find it down the well. But the streets...' Skwee swallowed hard. 'They're filled with nasty zombies, aren't they? And his lair will be crawling with guards...'

Xenixala smiled. 'Don't you worry about that. Just leave them to us.'

'See you later, guys,' said Larry as he retreated into the corner. 'Good luck!'

'You're coming too,' said Rose.

'Me?' said Larry. 'Go… outside?'

'Without Eric, we need all the help we can get,' Rose said as she readjusted her straps. 'We can't just leave Eric, either. He could wander off and eat someone. And the shop won't be safe for you much longer, anyway.'

'Ah…okay.' Larry made a gulping sound, which didn't make sense as Eric was inside what you'd assume was his throat. 'Lead the way, and I'll follow.'

'Right,' said Rose. 'Let's kill some dead.'

24

The shop became a haze of red and black. There were figures there... Eric could smell them. He could almost taste them.

Their delicious, fresh brains.

He tried to reach for one, but his arms did not respond. A force trapped him. Making him move. Making him walk.

His stomach growled.

He needed to eat.

He needed to feast.

Brains would do nicely. They wouldn't even need to be cooked. That would be a bonus. Those figures didn't need their brains. He could have a nibble. They wouldn't even notice. Maybe he could take a finger... or two.

Or a lung.

Or bbrrains.

How was he moving? They were all outside now. He felt the fresh air on his face. But only his face. His body was warm and snug.

The figures made noises at him. All he heard were muffles and grunts.

Where were they going? It didn't matter. Moving brought him closer to dinner.

Yummy... bbbrrraains.

'Eric, are you there?'

A voice. It pierced his skull from within.

'Eric, it's me, Felina.'

Will Felina tell him where to find bbbbrrrraaains?

'Please listen. You must resist the curse before your mind is completely gone. I can help you. I can fight it. But only for so long.'

If he fought the figures, he could have their bbbbbrrrrraaaains.

'I can help you when the time is right. But you need to be strong. Resist the hunger.'

The hunger.

'Resist...'

What was he thinking? Eating his friends? He could see clearly now. They were in the streets of Porkhaven.

There were so many zombies. Hundreds. Swarming all around.

He was going to become one.

He already *was* one.

But the smell. The fresh meat... right beside him.

Must... resist... the delicious...

Bbbbbbrrrrrraaaaains.

Bbbbbbbrrrrrrraaaaa

Ains.

Bb…bbbbb…b
Rr…rrrrrraa…aaaa
ai…ns.

25

Skilled Shaman Xenixala of Xendor, Harbinger of The Many Fates, Explorer of the Overlight, and Sponsor of *The Charitable Ooze Foundation For Missing Oozes,* frowned at the mess in the streets from her rooftop view. The moon sat high in the sky, casting a dim light across the peaks of the clustered houses and towers.

Porkhaven was home. It was an immutable force that weathered any storm. The gutters, windows, stone, alleys, shops, and pubs breathed and flowed together like a bad poem.

To see it become like this was an abomination.

The shambling masses filled the city as far as the eye could see, and her vampire vision saw further than ever before. Now, there were more undead than there were cobblestones. A filthy zombieland.

She leapt down and landed beside her new companions. They were, quite possibly, the oddest selection of adventuring cohorts she'd ever had the displeasure of teaming up with. How had it come to this? A zombie piloted by a mimic, a weakling goblin minion and a precocious little Westerner with a backpack full of tricks. It was as if some over-imaginative gods intentionally forced the most outrageous things upon her simply for their own amusement. Gods that told stories to other gods as some kind of game.

'How bad is it?' asked Rose.

'As bad as it could be,' said Xenixala, scowling as she dusted off the gutter grime from her robe. 'Just about every one of Porkhaven's citizens and adventurers are on the streets. And none of them are alive.'

'Can you see a safe route to the well Skwee told us about?' said Rose. 'The secret entrance to Edwardius's lair?'

'Easy,' said Xenixala. 'It's only a few blocks away. There are routes with fewer zombies, but there will still be plenty to contend with.' Xenixala laughed. 'Entering a dungeon through a secret passage hidden in an innocuous part of the city. Textbook adventuring.'

'We're *not* going into a dungeon,' said Rose sternly. 'This isn't an adventure. If it were, we'd need a licence.'

'Take it up with The King,' said Xenixala, rolling her eyes. 'Lucky for you, I count as a minion. Adventuring as a vampire has its perks.'

'This *isn't* an adventure.' Rose practically stamping her feet. 'We are doing our duty to protect the city and its people.'

'*Semantics.*' Xenixala scoffed. 'Everything is an adventure when I'm around.'

'Agree to disagree.'

'I agree that you should agree with me,' said Xenixala. 'Now, let's get moving before the sun comes up. Follow me.'

Rose huffed and said nothing.

Xenixala led them north, turning down a side street she'd seen from above.

Sometimes, a problematic party of adventurers just needed a firm hand. Adventurers didn't really want true freedom. They secretly wanted to be told what to do while feeling in control. If left to their own devices, the wrong kind of party would spend hours agonising over whether to open a door.

Six zombies shambled towards them: three bakers and three milkmaids. Their aprons tattered and stained, their faces half rotten. One baker dragged an oversized rolling pin along behind him. The narrow side street meant no escape.

Xenixala sighed. 'I'll deal with this.'

She flung into action.

In a heartbeat, she sliced two in half. Their bodies exploded in a mess of congealed blood.

She dashed at the next, swinging her claws. They cut like butter. Ironically, against a baker. He toppled. Head rolling.

The others fell just as easily.

She turned to see Rose and Skwee gawping at her. Larry's face was an unreadable metal visor. Eric groaned and gnashed.

'You looked like you enjoyed that,' said Rose. Her metal backpack chugged in the silence of the lane.

Xenixala had to admit it—she did. In the past, fighting minions as weak as that would have bored her. Now, it filled her with delight. Feasting on her victims afterwards would have been a bonus, but these didn't look especially fresh.

Perhaps being a vampire wasn't so bad after all. Wordsworth did seem quite happy in his library. That was where books belonged.

No.

She needed to get to Edwardius and not simply to catch up on old times.

Edwardius was a powerful necromancer now, powerful enough to raise an entire *city* of the dead. He was her best chance at getting Wordsworth back. She might even have the opportunity to apologise to him. If that failed, stopping him would improve her reputation. Enhancing her reputation would put an end to people hunting her at night.

She reached into her robe and felt the tiny scrap of Wordsworth's pages. She ran it between her fingers.

Only the most experienced necromancer would do.

But maybe it was all a waste of time. Perhaps she was better off as a vampire. Perhaps this was the life of misery she deserved. The blood called to her, even now. Who was she to deny herself that...

'Are you okay?' Rose looked at her with a quizzical expression. 'You're just standing there looking at a wall.'

'I'm fine,' said Xenixala. 'I'm always fine. We should move on.'

'I think the well is one block this way,' said Skwee, pointing.

'I *know*, goblin,' said Xenixala, changing direction. She stopped when she saw what lay down the next street.

The zombies filled every inch. These had weapons and armour. These were the adventuring kind.

At the front stood a great male barbarian with huge chunks missing from his chest, revealing a stilled heart through his rib cage. Beside him stood an elfen rogue in tattered black, wielding two daggers. Next to that—a female cleric, her once-white surcoat now caked in dried blood. They all raised their weapons and hissed.

If Xenixala didn't know any better, she could have sworn they were Blade, Panella and Gronk, the adventuring party she'd had to dispatch the other day. It was hard to say for sure. Their faces were too contorted and grey.

The wall of zombies sprung into action.

They ran faster than ever before.

They were on her.

She dived under an axe swung by the barbarian, then came up, swiping at his stomach. His intestines spilled out onto the ground. But he kept moving and swung again.

Skwee screamed. He hid behind Larry, who had four zombies trying to bite him. The zombies fell away, retching, their teeth shattered.

Rose's claw darted side to side, parrying swords and daggers whilst cutting off the heads of anyone who came too close.

Xenixala felt a bolt pierce her chest. She stumbled back.

Her chest sparkled. Magic.

She looked up to see a rotting mage. His hand was glowing green with an arcane light.

Another lightning bolt hit her. She rolled under two knights as they slashed their halberds.

Her chest oozed. She could have been killed.

She chanted a spell of her own.

A nova spread from her fingers. The wave blasted the zombies back. But only for a moment. They pressed forward again.

Xenixala cursed under her breath. It was easier to remember spells with Wordsworth around. A missile of magic, that's an easy one.

The missile of magic bolted three zombies right between the eyes. Their heads erupted into a mist of blood.

The cleric struck with her mace, hitting Xenixala on the shoulder. It crunched.

The pain shot through her whole body. A kind she hadn't felt in years.

A holy mace. Enchanted against the undead.

She would have laughed at the irony if it hadn't hurt so much. Undead wielding anti-undead weapons.

Xenixala bore her claws into the cleric's face until it was dead.

More zombies came.

She retreated behind Larry, casting a heal undead charm on herself. Her chest felt warm as the blood dried and healed. She sighed. It was usually a "cause wounds" charm, but she quickly learned it healed vampires.

Skwee jumped back as a warrior thrust her sword between his legs. Xenixala leapt upon her, slicing her torso in twain. The zombie warrior's armour was aesthetically pleasing but was barely enough to cover her oversized chest.

Xenixala's claws glanced off her. Somehow, she only managed to strike the tiny bit of metal that barely covered the zombie's nipples.

Xenixala swore. Magical armour was cheating.

The warrior attacked again with her sword. Xenixala leapt aside, but only just in time.

Rose's claw stabbed the warrior in the head.

Xenixala grunted in gratitude and wiped the mess from her eyes. Rose winked at her and returned to the carnage.

After what felt like hours, they cleared the alleyway. So many bodies littered the floor that walking without squelching on something was impossible. Xenixala made a mental note to burn her shoes later.

She was surprised at the strength of those zombies. If she hadn't had the power and speed of a vampire, she would certainly have been dead. Although, her magic would have been more potent with Wordsworth around.

Xenixala noticed a glint hidden amongst the debris. She knelt and scooped the piece from the warrior's body. She wiped off the red mulch to read the inscription: *The Breastplate of Hellfire.* Not bad. Maybe she could pawn it off at a *"Sword's 'N Stuff".* It would likely be worth something.

They reached the well on the next street over. The sorry excuse for a water source sat in the centre of a small square, surrounded by nondescript houses. The well had a little wooden roof coated in moss over a round stone base. A chain dangled from the winch down to the darkness below.

Skwee jumped with joy when he saw it. 'There it is!' he said with glee. 'This should lead us into his lair. I told you it was close!'

'Licence and registration please.' Came a voice.

Not this again

A spirit hovered over the well with a clipboard. He shimmered a translucent blue with an amorphous form that vaguely resembled a human.

'What do you mean?' said Rose. 'There isn't a new water tax, is there?'

'Don't be ridiculous,' said the spirit. 'This is for the *adventuring* tax.'

'But we're *not* adventures,' said Rose, folding her arms. 'We're here to save the city.'

'Sounds pretty adventurery to me,' said the spirit. 'Listen, I don't make the rules. You'll need to show me some kind of identification. We can't have vigilantes running around blowing things up and murdering people. The city would be in chaos.'

'It's *already* in chaos!' exclaimed Rose, waving her arms. 'Look around you! This is the only way to the necromancer's lair. Once we stop him…'

The spirit cut her off. 'Invading a necromancer's lair to save the kingdom? That sounds like a textbook adventure to me.'

'But you *have* to let us pass!'

'I'm afraid I can't do that. Section four-six-two-three The King's new decree states that…'

'Why you no good, trolls tooth, son of a…'

'Just doing my job, ma'am.'

Xenixala cleared her throat. 'Let me handle this.' She strode over to the spirit and looked him dead in the eye. Or at least where she assumed his eyes would be. 'We are a band of minions and, therefore, do not require a licence. I am a vampire.' She paused and bared her fangs. 'This is a zombie inside a mimic.' She gestured at Larry. 'And that is, quite clearly, a goblin.'

'I am,' said Skwee.

'Brrauuuuuhhhns,' groaned Eric.

'She's not wrong,' said Larry.

'Ah, I see,' said the spirit checking his clipboard. 'My apologies. Please continue with your minion work. And thank you for your service.'

He disappeared in a puff of smoke.

'See, that wasn't so hard, was it?' said Xenixala.

Rose frowned. 'How did that spirit know about this entrance?'

Xenixala inspected the well's chain. It felt slick with mould. 'I'm sure there's magic to tell them where to find adventurers. But I wouldn't think about it too much, or it might give you a headache.'

26

Skwee jumped from the chain at the bottom of the well and splashed into the icy water. He shivered. He could hardly believe that he was back. Something about the damp smell and dim light spoke to him in a way he couldn't explain.

A cry came from above.

He ducked.

Larry crashed beside him, cascading water all around.

'Sorry,' said Larry. 'I'm still getting used to having limbs. They're awfully strange things.'

Eric groaned from inside his armoured prison. Skwee hoped the fall hadn't hurt his fragile human bones. If they ever changed him back from zombiehood, Eric would be livid if he wasn't in one piece.

They clambered out of the water and into the passageway that led off from it. They both shook the water from themselves.

'Alright down there?' Rose's voice echoed from high above.

'Fine, thanks!' Skwee called back.

Naturally, as the bravest of the group, Skwee had been sent first to check for zombies, traps, or other miscellaneous dangers. Skwee had to admit it was an excellent idea and was more than happy to oblige.

A moment later, Rose arrived, clambering down the walls of the well with her claw.

Xenixala appeared beside him out of nowhere. 'Out of my way, goblin,' she said.

'Did you see that bat?' asked Skwee, stepping aside.

Rose dusted herself off and produced a metal ball from her backpack. She held it aloft, and it glowed a warm yellow light. 'Shall we?'

They continued down the passageway, Rose's orb illuminating their path. Judging by the marks, the tunnel walls were roughly hewn by goblins not too long ago. Larry's clanking footsteps gently echoed while Rose's backpack chugged along.

'I can't smell any zombies,' said Skwee with relief.

'Nor can I,' said Xenixala. 'But I can smell goblin.' She glared at Skwee. 'And not just this one here.'

'Goblins we can handle,' whispered Rose. 'So long as they don't sound the alarm, we'll be okay. We have to keep quiet, or we could be swarmed.'

The tunnel ceiling angled lower and lower. Eventually, Rose, Xenixala and Larry had to crawl, resulting in a strange muttering sound. Skwee thought this was the perfect height.

The small tunnel soon connected with a human-sized one, allowing the party to clamber back to their full height. Like in any good evil overlord's lair, dark wall hangings and nondescript torches adorned the walls. It even *smelled* like an evil lair—a mix of fresh goblin sweat and dust. Skwee thought it was delightful.

Rose looked left and right. 'Which way is it to The Doom Device, Skwee?'

Skwee felt an overwhelming pressure on his chest as if an invisible bugbear was crushing him. All of them were relying on Skwee. He couldn't let them down. If he did, Eric would be a zombie forever. They first needed to destroy the Doom Device to stop any further spread of Edwardius' curse through *The Elixir of Death*. The device also somehow kept Edwardius alive.

'Umm...' Skwee stammered. He flipped a coin in his head. 'Left. I think.'

They continued down the long passageway. After a few minutes, they came to a doorway with a sign over it that read—*"Goblin Resources"* in splattered green paint.

'Ah, I know the way from here!' Skwee exclaimed.

Xenixala tutted. 'You mean you didn't know the way before?'

'I knew I knew it. I just didn't know for sure. You know?'

'No.' The others said in unison.

'Well, anyway,' Skwee continued, 'If we go right here, we should come to...' He pointed at the ceiling and let his finger follow along. 'There! You see that pipe? We follow the pipes.'

'If you say so,' said Xenixala.

'I have faith in you, Skwee,' Rose said, patting him on the head.

As they continued, the pipes converged to become one. The great pipe oozed brown-green slime between its seams.

'It's a little too quiet here for my liking,' said Xenixala. 'Where are all the minions? There should be more guards than this.'

'They run a tight ship down here,' said Skwee sagely. 'There's a strict delegation hierarchy, with a schedule that's set months in advance. Today is wash day, so most guards are cleaning their uniforms.'

They arrived at a doorway cut into the rock face. The great pipe merged with the wall beside it.

'Here we are,' said Skwee in a whisper. 'Remember, The Doom Device's valve at the top is the weak spot. If we twist it off, it should self-destruct.'

'Excellent,' said Xenixala. 'Let's get on with it then.' She pushed past Skwee and opened the door.

A giant green-glowing copper vat sat in the middle of the cavern, hundreds of pipes snaking out of it and across the walls. The Doom Device. In matching uniforms, goblins hurried to and fro carrying vials, clipboards and tools. They splashed across the puddles on the stone floor.

One figure stood out amongst the goblins, as he was about three times their height. He wore a top hat and a thin moustache sat where his nose ought to have been were he not an orc. His outfit matched the other goblins: the traditional black tunic with a splash of acid green. He lashed a long black whip at one of the passing minions. There was a loud *crack* and a yelp.

'Get back to work, *little one*. We don't want to disappoint our *master,* do we?' Catch turned to them as they entered the room and lowered his whip. 'Skwee?' he said. 'They've been looking *everywhere* for you. Edwardius has been *awfully* worried.' He noticed the others and licked his lips. 'And you have some new recruits, I see... *Very good.*'

'Oh, uh, hello, Catch,' Skwee stammered. 'Nice to see you again.' His body froze. This was the creature who took him. The one who brought him here. He wanted to scream, but his mouth wouldn't move. Every fibre of his body wanted to conform, to obey. Don't stand out from the crowd. Do what they say. Don't make a fuss.

Rose looked at Catch, then back at Skwee. Her face seemed sad. 'Did this orc... hurt you, Skwee?'

Skwee slowly nodded.

'That's all you had to say,' said Xenixala, resolute. She flicked her wrist.

A fireball exploded.

Catch fell back, ablaze. He shrieked and flailed his limbs, hopelessly fighting the flames.

The other goblins looked on in horror, perfectly still.

Catch fell to the ground, silent except for the sizzle and pop of embers. His whip clattered by his side.

'Friends!' Skwee announced.

All eyes were on him.

'Goblins,' Skwee continued. 'Countryfolk. Listen up. Edwardius is a cruel master. We were all brought here and kept without pay. This is what humans call *sleevery.*'

Rose cleared her throat. 'It's *slavery.*'

'Ah, yes, *slavery*. We do all the work but get none of the rewards. They take advantage of our nice nature. But no more! Now you are free!'

Silence.

One of the taller goblins stepped forward. 'But... where will we go? It's warm here.'

There was a murmur of agreement amongst the other goblins.

'And there's free food,' said another.

More murmurs.

'And we have a purpose. Don't forget the sense of purpose.'

The murmurs grew even louder.

'Alright, well,' said Skwee, scratching his head. 'Besides the warmth, food and sense of purpose, you also don't have freedom.'

'Freedom is overrated,' said the goblin. 'It's safe here and we like it. Why did you have to come along and ruin our great gig? I'd rather be a manager here than begging for scraps on the streets of Porkhaven. That 'ain't freedom; that's oppression.'

The goblins' murmurs became deafening.

They made a good point. Skwee was lucky to have a lovely home to go to with friends and hot dinners. Skwee fiddled with the hem of his shirt. 'I um…well…'

What would Eric do? Eric always knew what to say to the minions. 'Well…' he started, 'These zombies will have killed many, many humans. So… there are going to be a lot of jobs going spare. You know? And houses, too, probably. So if we stop the master… you can live in Porkhaven like a human. It'll be lovely.'

Rose had told him that once they stopped Edwardius, everyone he'd cursed to become a zombie would return to life. However, they'd had to kill quite a few zombies, not to mention that most seemed to be missing rather a lot of body parts or essential organs. So he didn't expect them to survive having their souls returned.

The goblins beamed and tittered amongst themselves.

'Not a bad point,' said the tall goblin. 'What do we have to do now then?'

'We need to set the self-destruct for the Doom Device here. Then you guys spread the word to the other goblins in the lair. Tell them to flee before this thing detonates.'

The goblins nodded to one another and then scampered off. Their laughter echoed down the halls.

'Well done, Skwee!' said Rose with a jump of joy. 'Eric would have enjoyed that.' She gestured over to Larry's metallic form, from where Eric hissed inside. 'I'll be sure to tell him about it once he's back to normal.'

Xenixala smiled. 'Surprisingly effective, little one. I like your style. Perfect manipulation.' She looked up at the huge copper vat. 'Now, let's get to this device. The top valve, did you say?'

Rose's claw reached the top of the Doom Device and snapped off the metal wheel that sat at its peak. Steam exploded with a colossal hiss. The ceiling's alarm runes glowed red, piercing the silence with a shrill tone.

'We don't have too long now,' said Skwee. 'We need to find Edwardius.'

'And I assume you know where he is?' asked Xenixala.

'Yes, he's on Level Ten,' said Skwee. 'It's his brooding spot, where he can cackle and rub his hands together. You can't miss it.'

27

Eric's stomach growled in protest.
Bbrraains.
Bb...bbbbb...b
Rr...rrrrrraa...aaaaai...ns.
Why am I not full of fresh flesh? It said. Some lovely liver. Or a kidney.
Or better yet... brrraaains.
There was nothing Eric could do to appease his stomach. He was trapped. No matter how much he thrashed and gnashed, no flesh came his way. He wasn't going to give up, though.
He continued to gnash.
You never know. If you try something enough times, it's bound to work eventually.
Gnash gnash.
The people following him around didn't pay him much attention. They were too busy chatting and moaning.
Gnash.
There was a short girl strapped to a metal box, a tiny green boy and a black-haired woman dressed in black. Why were they following him?
The green boy spoke. 'This is it, the door to Edwardius' brooding spot.' The boy stopped and pointed at a big brown thing—presumably a door.
'What's with the boxes?' said the black-haired woman. 'Is that a...?'
'Greetings adventurers,' said a little hairy man behind a wooden box. There was a green sign, but Eric didn't understand the strange symbols splattered onto it. 'Can I interest you in some of my wares? I have the finest swords in the land.'
Maybe the shop would sell brains. If Eric gnashed hard enough, they might get the message.
Gnash, gnash, gnash.
'That's handy,' said the half-robot girl. We could use some supplies before we face Edwardius.'
'Perhaps a little *too* handy,' said the woman in black. 'Gnome, who told you to set up shop here? This location cannot be economically viable for you.'
The shopkeeper smiled. 'Why, the dark overlord of this establishment, of course! The New Master. Eggwartuis? He informed me that a band of adventurers would come along eventually. Something about a nemesis? Looks like he was right.'
'That's true,' said the little green boy with the pointy ears. 'The overlord training seminars were very particular about refreshment

locations for a successful fight with a nemesis. Or something. It never made much sense to me.'

'*Please* buy something,' said the gnome. 'Or I'll be out of business. My family is starving. You're my first customer since I moved here.'

'Alright, then,' said the girl. 'What do you have?'

'Wonderful!' The gnome jumped up and down. 'Can I interest you in a large number of basic rusty daggers? I picked them up from an adventurer a while ago and can't seem to shift 'em.'

'What are we supposed to do with those?'

'Make a necklace or something? I also have a lovely quarterstaff. If that's your kind of thing?'

'What kind of quarterstaff?'

'You know. Half of half a staff.'

'Oh.'

'I also have an eighthstaff, but that might be a bit too small. Very good for fairies, mind you.'

'Um, don't you have any powerful armour, swords, or anything? Maybe some potions?'

'Hmm... I was hoping you'd have gone for the rusty daggers and staffs... How about a wheel of cheese?'

'Offer us something of value or leave us be, gnome,' spat the woman in black.

Eric agreed. Sell them some brains.

'Alright, alright. How about a Potion of Lightness?'

'Interesting, what does it do?'

'Makes you lighter.'

'I see.'

'Just be careful, or you might float away. If I were you, I'd keep a rope handy.'

'Alright, fine. We'll take it.'

'And the wheel of cheese,' said the girl. 'I'm starving.'

'And the wheel of cheese.'

'Excellent!' said the gnome with delight. 'That'll be fifteen gold pieces.'

Eric gnashed harder, but they still didn't get the message. Not cheese. *Brains*.

'Good luck!' the gnome shouted after them as they walked over to the door.

'Look!' said the girl. 'There's a sign on the door. It says, "*Warning. Trap ahead. The New Master is not liable for any damages caused. Enter at your own risk.*"'

The woman in black tutted. 'It's a bluff. No one would be stupid enough to signpost a trap like that.' She pushed the door open.

The green boy hesitated. 'Um, don't be so sure about that...'

Eric's prison lumbered after the figures and in through the open doorway.

The world went upside down.
Rope lashed around them.
Gnash.
Rushing upwards.
Screams.
Gnash.
'We're trapped!' shrieked the girl.
Eric could only see a boot. Rope pushed it against his face.
Gnash, gnash.
'Ow! Who bit me?'
Music began to play. It was soothing, almost beautiful. What was he doing? Why was he upside down? Why was Rose's boot in his mouth?
'Ah, Skwee,' boomed a deep, rasping voice. 'I see you have brought them to me, just as I asked. *Excellent* work, time for a promotion, I think...'

28

Skwee watched his friends fly into the air, wrapped in a rope net. Suspended high above the chamber, they swung gently and cursed violently.

It was a classic evil overlord booby trap. Skwee had dodged thousands of similar contraptions and been caught in a thousand more. Something deep inside his brain had kicked in, meaning he'd leapt aside just in time. The warning sign had also been a clue.

Beside them, corpses hung from the ceiling on long chains. Great vats lined the walls, glowing green and full of odd body parts. The stench felt so familiar that Skwee didn't need to cover his nose any more. A tiny orchestra of goblins frantically played tunes in the room's far corner. This was for maximum dramatic effect. Skwee had got to know a few of the goblins in that band and thought they were all very talented, with the exception of the oboe player.

Edwardius slowly clapped. His rotting face beamed as he looked up at his catch. He stood from his throne of bones and walked towards them, his rusted black paladin armour creaking as he moved.

'Ah, Skwee,' said Edwardius, his voice gravelly and strained. 'I see you have brought them to me, just as I asked. *Excellent* work, time for a promotion, I think…'

Skwee smiled. Edwardius did like him. Only a few people liked him, so he had to take any opportunity he could when they did.

Xenixala raged. 'I *knew* that weasel goblin wasn't to be trusted!' She writhed and shot magical sparks. She screamed as the spells ricocheted back onto herself.

'Don't try to escape, *fools*,' said Edwardius, with all the spite Skwee had told him to employ in such circumstances. He'd also told him to insult people with the word "fools" as much as possible. It was an excellent and child-friendly way to belittle an adventurer or underling. 'The rope has an anti-magic aura. I am *very* prepared, as I have been… expecting you.'

Skwee walked over to Edwardius. Hopefully, his plan would work, and Edwardius wouldn't give him a fate worse than a fate worse than death, as he had promised.

'Finally, I shall have my vengeance!' Edwardius cackled and rubbed his wrinkled hands together.

Skwee cleared his throat and whispered to him. 'Remember to laugh a little louder. It's more menacing.'

'Ah yes, good point, Skwee.' He laughed again, and it echoed around the hall.

Skwee gave him the thumbs up.

'*Xenixala*,' Edwardius spat on the ground, then glared up at the helpless band. 'Oh, how I have waited for this moment. *You* did this to me. *You* created me.' He flicked back his droopy white hair. 'You... are my... *nemesis*.' He closed his eyes and held up a clenched fist.

Skwee had heard Edwardius recite this speech in the mirror many times. He had absolutely nailed the pitch.

'It's uh... good to see you again, Edwardius,' said Xenixala from up high.

'And I am no longer *Edwardius*,' said Edwardius, as if saying his own name was a dirty curse word. 'They call me... *The New Master.*'

Xenixala scoffed. 'Who calls you that?'

'People.'

'People you employ?'

'Yes, and others too. Lots of people do.'

'If you say so... wait, did you say *nemesis*?'

'Indeed I did, *witch*.'

Skwee had begun to wonder if being called a witch was an insult, considering how much spite Edwardius employed in using the word. Skwee thought witches were generally well-liked, as they fulfilled a vital role in society as healers, potion brewers and cat breeders. But perhaps he was wrong.

Xenixala snorted. 'Nemesis is a bit dramatic, isn't it? I hardly think about you at all.'

Edwardius' face scrunched, making his open sores weep with green goo. 'There isn't a *moment* that I don't think of you! Not after what you did to me...'

'I didn't do anything. You attacked *me*. It was self-defence.'

Edwardius shook with rage. 'You are the *wretch* that stood between us and The Dark Master. I only *just* survived. It was pure luck that my head flew into the Elixir vat... and I regenerated into the form you see before you.' He looked down at himself. 'But not fully. You *destroyed* both me and my beloved Felina.'

A figure shambled into the light. Skin dripped from her tiny pixie frame, her pointed features warped and green. Flies buzzed around her head as she lurched.

Poor Felina, it didn't seem like much of a life. Or unlife, for that matter. If Eric stayed as a zombie, perhaps they could be friends.

'Felina. My beloved.' Edwardius shook his head. 'Look what has become of her. The vats were not so kind to her as they were to me.'

Felina stopped suddenly with a *clank*, the chain around her neck holding her still. She wheezed and stretched out her arms, helplessly clawing towards them.

'She is all I have left, yet she is death itself.' He wiped a drip from his eyelid. 'Soon, everyone will know my pain. The zombie curse is crude, yet effective. I can control my hordes or leave them to roam free, spreading the curse with each bite. Growing my strength effortlessly...'

Skwee loved a good monologue, but this one needed some work. It was awfully expositional.

'Very clever.' Xenixala yawned. 'And now you're half life and half death you want to inflict across the land blah blah...'

'Not *blah blah!*' Edwardius cut in. 'You're ruining my speech! Where was I? Ah yes... You are the wretch that stood between us and The Dark Master...'

'Get on with it, already,' snapped Xenixala. 'Just let me down so we can have a proper final showdown.'

'Ha! You would like that, wouldn't you? That, however, is the one piece of advice I won't be taking from the Evil Overlord Guide. I'm no *fool*. I think it would be wiser to complete my plan of domination and *then* have you executed. There's a vat of acid over there with your name on it.'

He gestured across the room, and sure enough, there was a vat with the words *"that nasty witch"* scratched onto the side. Skwee wondered what the chemicals were. An open vat like that would surely have breached about a dozen health and safety codes.

'Um, Edwardius...' said Rose, her voice wavering and unseen behind the blob of bodies. 'I mean... The New Master, sir? Eric, Larry and I didn't do any of that stuff to you... and we don't actually know Xenixala all that well... and so, um... maybe you could let us go?'

Edwardius shook his head. 'You aided and abetted the witch. You are *equally* responsible.' He drew a deep breath. 'I understand now why tracking you down has been so hard, *Xenixala*. I see you have become a vampire. You have no soul to trace. So now you are undead, like me. We are not so dissimilar, you and I...'

Skwee agreed on their similarities. They certainly had similar egos, at least. Announcing this comparison to a nemesis was also crucial for improving a bond, thus making for a more epic showdown.

'I am nothing like you,' said Xenixala. 'Hold on a second... are you wearing eyeliner?'

Edwardius froze. 'I'll have you know, it's called *guyliner*.'

'And is that a goatee?'

'Skwee said it made me look more imposing...'

'It's tragically wispy. I wouldn't take fashion tips from goblins.'

Skwee agreed. He wouldn't take fashion advice from himself either. For some reason, people weren't so keen burlap sacks and rotten loincloths.

'*Enough*!' Edwardius screamed.

The chamber fell silent, only punctuated by the gentle gnashing sounds from Eric and Felina.

Skwee readied himself. The humans almost certainly thought he had betrayed them. Skwee didn't like upsetting them like that, but he had no choice. Edwardius had to believe it, which meant it had to look convincing. He'd forgotten about the net trap and had to improvise. Improvising was important in any plan. Overlord or adventurer. He learned that in Section Three of the training.

It was now or never.

Skwee cleared his throat. 'Uh...Rose?'

'Yes, Skwee?' said Rose.

'Remember what we bought at the shop outside the door?'

'The wheel of cheese?'

'Uh, no, the other thing.'

'Oh, right, yeah.'

'Maybe take a drink?'

'Gotcha.'

'Wait, what's happening?' Edwardius looked at him quizzically. 'What do you mean?'

'Oh, it was a... poison,' said Skwee. 'So they can die.'

'Ah, very considerate of you, Skwee. But actually, I'd rather they die slowly and painfully if possible.'

'My mistake, master. Um. Please excuse me while I go over to the net-release lever.'

'Be my guest... anyway, as I was saying... Wait, why are they floating upwards?'

With that, Skwee pulled the lever.

29

Optimus Occultist Xenixala of Xendor, Discoverer of The Lost Temple of Stox-Ku, Haunter of The Dragon Dream, and the only woman known to be able to lick her own elbow, grinned as Rose drank the Potion of Lightness. The effect was instantaneous. Rose shot upward, bringing the net and trapped party with her. They clunked onto the rough stone ceiling. Xenixala laughed, Larry yelped, Eric groaned and Rose gasped.

Xenixala had been too quick to judge the cunning little goblin. Skwee knew how to play Edwardius like a fiddle. And the tune was their freedom.

Skwee pulled a lever and the net fell away.

Xenixala was prepared and thought: *'hiss'*. She transformed into a bat and fluttered from her confines. She'd tried to do it earlier, but something about the rope had even warded against transmutation. It must have been worth a small fortune.

Larry and Eric were not so lucky. They fell with the net and crashed to the floor. Fortunately, mimics were hardy creatures, as they had to imitate solid steel and wood. Eric probably broke a few bones, but he was technically already dead.

Rose remained pinned to the ceiling, the potion giving her a faint blue glow. Her backpack sprung to life, steam whizzing and claw whirring.

'What in the?!' Edwardius raged. 'Skwee! What have you done!'

'I'm sorry, master,' Skwee whimpered, backing away. 'But you're actually not my master... not really. Eric is.'

'And who in Mole's name is *Eric*?'

'The human about to bite you...' said Skwee as Larry lunged at Edwardius.

Eric gnashed.

Edwardius cried out, grappling with the duo.

Xenixala landed and transformed back into vampire form. If she ever became human again, she would have to find a similar spell. Flapping about as a bat was surprisingly handy.

Rose's claw extended from her vantage above. It snatched at Edwardius' head, tearing out chunks of hair and scalp.

Edwardius roared, forcing Larry back with a mighty swipe. He turned and ran to the end of the room.

'You think such puny creatures can best me?' He cackled, then pulled on a great chain. It rattled and clunked as the green vats began to drain. Xenixala stepped away as the foul fluid gushed across the cobbles.

Fortunately, the zombie messes had already ruined her shoes.

The glass shattered. Strange figures emerged from the vats. They looked as if someone had chopped up a dozen adventurers, jumbled them around, then glued them back together but then gone off for lunch and left them to rot in the sun.

Four abominations. A tiny pixie frame atop stunted dwarven legs with barbarian's arms sprouting from sorcerer robes. A lizard-faced paladin with tiny claws and long elfen legs. A six-headed, four-armed rogue wielding four halberds. And a centaur with a horse's head. Flesh dripped from their rotting armour. Flies furiously buzzed around them. They moaned and shambled forward.

'Behold!' Edwardius proclaimed, 'My beautiful creations! The *perfect* adventurers. Ready to match the "*great*" Xenixala.' He performed the air quotes with as much emphasis as was humanly possible. 'Finally, I will see you *dead*. You've evaded my assassins for the last time!'

By this point, it was unsurprising for Xenixala to hear that Edwardius had sent the assassins after her. Although, for some reason, it didn't give her any relief. It felt empty. As if she'd heard that somebody had invented a new texture of porridge. She thought the knowledge would give her a sense of security. But deep down, she knew it was meaningless. She had wronged so many people and done so many misdeeds that it didn't matter who it was. Someone would come after her eventually. She would have to pay the price.

If she remained a vampire, perhaps she'd stand a chance at fending off the next disgruntled acquaintance.

She ducked as a halberd swung.

The abominations were upon them.

She muttered a spell, and an orb of energy fizzled around her.

Lightning exploded as it hit the energy field. The sorcerer creature shrieked with confusion and cast its spell again. The spell bounced back and hit the thing in the shoulder, causing it to scream even louder. Xenixala put her hands over her ears.

Rose, still on the ceiling, threw down metallic spheres. They clattered at the feet of the paladin, who tried to pick them up, but its arms were too small to reach. The balls exploded in its face. Smoke and mucus swirled into the air.

Larry ran at the rogue. The suit of amour had no weapons, so he leapt onto his foe, arms outstretched. He grasped with a mighty bear hug while Eric bit and tore. The rogue dropped its halberds and pushed back with four twisted arms.

There was a yelp. Xenixala turned to see Skwee hiding under a table. The horse-headed centaur bayed at him.

She sighed.

'*Sweetio blokkuis!*' she called out, pointing. A pile of sugar cubes appeared at the centaur's hooves. It seemed startled initially, then turned its attention away from Skwee and nuzzled into the treats.

Skwee smiled and mouthed a thank you towards her.

She felt a tingle run through her. Almost warmth.

Larry flew across the room. He shattered against the wall, his armour-shape buckled. The four-armed rogue roared, then turned its attention to Xenixala.

She turned into a bat as the beast swung at her. Flapping away, she felt smug.

Too smug.

The rogue snatched her from the air. It brought her towards its gaping mouth, its breath a haze of rancid meat.

She transferred back into a vampire. '*Fooseroll dah!*' she cried. The spell sent the monster flying back, skittering across the floor.

Rose tumbled down, no longer glowing. Xenixala caught her fall with an enchanted hand spell.

'Thanks,' said Rose, hopping off. 'I owe y…'

Rose exploded in a ball of lightning. Xenixala winced at the blinding light.

The mutant sorcerer screeched with delight.

Rose groaned from the ground, her backpack wheezing.

'Eat the cheese,' said Xenixala, dodging another lightning bolt. 'The wheel of cheese. It'll heal you.'

Rose frowned but complied. Her blackened arm reached for her satchel and pulled out the wheel of cheese. She took a small bite as she lay on the floor.

Xenixala turned to face the sorcerer.

She flicked her wrist, and a fireball shot forward. The flames exploded on the spellcaster, and the smoke cleared, revealing them unharmed.

Edwardius cackled from the corner, enjoying the show. Overlords always kept their hands clean while their minions fought.

Magic wouldn't do. She needed raw power.

The power of a vampire.

Her fangs distended. She charged.

Lightning flew. She batted it away. Lightning flew again. She ignored the pain.

She leapt onto the sorcerer, tearing with her claws. Ribbons of flesh danced. Black blood sprayed.

The creature fell. The floor puddles splashed.

Her heart pulsed. How could she deny herself such a thrill? She was a hunter now, after all. She licked her lips and turned to the final creature. The rogue clambered to its feet. It picked up the halberds and spun them into an endless swirl of blades.

Xenixala dashed at it, weaving to and fro. The halberds swiped and slashed. She bent in mid-air, turning into a bat, then back again, now behind the abomination. She swiped with her claws. They glanced off the hardened skin.

She cursed, then murmured the words.

Her claws glowed with a new spell. They sizzled as they cut again, deep through the pallid flesh.

She choked at the stench as she jumped away. It was like barbecued toenails. The beast crumpled, split asunder.

Xenixala stood panting. She felt strong. How could she give up this much power?

Larry whined from the ground, unable to stand. His limbs bent in ways they shouldn't. Rose had eaten half of the cheese yet remained charred and floor-bound. Skwee snivelled from behind his table.

The undead Felina rattled her chains, wildly clawing at the air.

A slow clap came from the end of the chamber.

Edwardius walked towards her. 'You think you can defeat me?' He smirked. 'I am *invincible*!'

Xenixala cleared her throat. 'We destroyed your Doom Device.'

'Oh, I see...' Edwardius hesitated. 'Well, I'm pretty certain I'm still invincible. My body is undead. The necromancer training said so.'

Xenixala grinned. 'Let's put that to the test then, shall we?' She extended her claws.

She needed to take Edwardius alive. He was the only necromancer powerful enough to get her soul back. To get Wordsworth back.

She bounded at him as he drew his sword.

But at what cost? The land was a ruinous mess of undead. Countless lives would be lost to The Underworld forever. Could she let Edwardius live?

They clashed. He thrust at her. He was fast. The blade cut deep. The icy steel went through her again. Her dark blood drizzled. She wrenched free, transforming into a bat. She fluttered behind him, back into a vampire. He spun to meet her. She parried his strike, her claws glowing. Sparks flew.

She'd already saved the land from the last evil master. Must it fall on her to do it again?

They brought this on themselves.

She brought this on them. Edwardius did this because of her. It was her mess. She should do the right thing. Shouldn't she?

She punctured his armour. His body felt cold as she tore at his insides. She flicked her wrist. Fire swelled with him. It exploded, sending them apart.

They circled one another, panting, eyes locked. They both dripped from their wounds, leaving a trail of entrails in their paths.

'You are my nemesis, and I yours,' said Edwardius through gritted teeth. 'We *need* each other. This fight will go on forever. Two immortals in an eternity of hate and suffering. My vengeance will be *endless*.'

He was enjoying this a little too much.

But how could she deny it? She was enjoying it, too. The thrill pulsed through her dead veins, bringing her life.

'Don't you have better things to do?' said Xenixala. 'Hating me forever is a waste of time. Why do you care?'

But it was her hatred that created him. Her negligence. Her carelessness. Of course he should hate her. Everyone should hate her. *She* hated her.

'I do it all for Felina.' Edwardius spat. 'She cannot enact her revenge, so I must do it for her.'

She had to make a choice.

He charged her again, eyes wide and full of rage.

30

Eric was furious.
No matter what he attacked, he never got any brains.
Juicy braaains.
He should give up at this point.
'Eric, can you hear me.'
He tried chewing the inside of his mouth, but the meat wasn't fresh—in fact, it was disgusting.
'Eric, you need to listen to me.'
He tumbled upside down several times and then was thrown across a room. What an awful day.
'It's Felina. Let me in. I can help you. You have to let me in.'
A door opened up inside him. A light glistened in his eye. Where was he? Why did he stink of mimic dung?
'Eric, you need to give Edwardius a message from me. Can you stand up?'
He pushed his way out of the crumpled suit of armour. It was wet in a way that metal wasn't. He looked down at his hands. His pale, rotting hands.
'Go to Edwardius, speak to him.'
How did walking work? It was as if he hadn't walked in years. His legs moved somehow—one foot, then another.
He shuffled forward.
That's it. Towards the brains.
If he stretched his arms out, he would reach the brains sooner.
'Focus, Eric. Tell Edwardius that Felina still loves you. Tell him this is folly.'
Eric reached the figures in the middle of the room.
They stopped fighting.
Eric tried to speak, but the words didn't come.
'Tell him...'
'E….dward…ius…' Eric rasped.
Edwardius looked at him. 'Ah,' he said. 'One of my thralls has come to my aid. Kill this witch, thrall.'
Something inside him made him want to comply.
But no.
Must resist… the… brains…
'Tell Edwardius that Felina still loves you.'
'Felina…' said Eric. 'Still… loves you.'
The mouths of the pair hung open.
'I know,' said Edwardius after a moment. 'And I, her.'
'I am… inside Eric,' said Eric, each word strained. 'He… found me... In The Underworld.'

'Impossible,' said Edwardius. 'This is a trick.' He looked across at Felina's corpse. It rattled its chains, nodding along with Eric's words.

'Let her go... Edwardius,' said Eric. 'Let yourself... go.'

A tear rolled down Edwardius' cheek. 'I cannot... this is my vengeance. *Our* vengeance.'

'She doesn't... need vengeance...' said Eric, 'You do. Go to her... Be with her.'

Felina stretched out her arms, groaning.

Edwardius bit his lip. 'I... but...'

'She is... in so much pain. You are both... in so much pain.'

Edwardius nodded resolutely. He strode over to Felina and they embraced. 'I'm sorry, my love.' He sobbed. 'I'm so sorry.'

The zombie pixie splatted in his arms as he crushed her.

He fell to his knees, head in hand.

'Thank you, Eric... His soul is free... His immortality is no more...'

The voice disappeared.

Edwardius remained still, coated in a mess of flesh.

Xenixala went over to him and put a hand on his shoulder.

His head hung, he whispered. 'Do what you must.'

With that, she cut off his head with a single swipe.

Overwhelming light.

Air.
Smells.
Feeling.
Rushing.

Gushing reality spun all around. Brightness. His lungs filled with freshness.

He fell to the floor. Every part of him tingled.

He felt... alive.

He was alive.

Eric stood up. His whole body ached in a way he never thought possible. He was in a chamber of sorts. His friends were there... and Xenixala. And a dead paladin. And a *lot* of mess. The floor was slick with brown and black sludge.

His mouth tasted like a bin in a graveyard. Why were his hands so white? He stumbled, but Rose caught him. Her overalls were scorched black, but her face beamed.

'Are you back, Eric?' she said. Her hold tightened on his arm.

'Yeah, I'm back,' he muttered. 'You smell like cheese.'

She hugged him. 'You are back!'

Larry had turned back into a wooden chest and slid over, trudging through the slush. 'I hope I kept you safe,' he said, his lid flapping wonkily. 'It was exhilarating.'

Skwee emerged from behind some rubble. 'Is it over?' he said sheepishly, eyes darting. 'Is he… dead-dead?'

Xenixala wiped her hands on her robes. 'He's no longer undead if that's what you mean. He's gone, which is all that matters.'

'You were amazing,' said Rose, smiling at Xenixala. 'I've never seen fighting like it.'

Xenixala sighed and turned away. 'Indeed.' There was a sadness in her voice that Eric had never heard from her before. 'He could have made me human again.'

It suddenly all made sense. That was why Xenixala wanted to find Edwardius with them. A necromancer to cure her affliction.

Xenixala was still one of life's greatest mysteries. She never seemed happy, yet always wanted more. At least Eric had the good sense never to be happy and only want less.

'I've lost my soul forever.' Xenixala shook her head. 'He was the greatest necromancer I've ever seen. Only someone that powerful could bring my soul back.'

Eric thought for a moment. Should he tell her? She had saved them, after all. Yet she seemed to hate them so much that he wanted to curse her name and never think of her again. But he was better than that.

'Don't be so sure,' said Eric. 'I may know just the person you need to speak to…'

31

Skwee readjusted his overalls and wiped off the breakfast crumbs, as the throne room doors opened before them. The guard told them to enter, so they did. The palace took his breath away the first time he had been inside it, but after The King had summoned them a dozen times, it all became rather mundane. Just another day on the job. All the plush red silks, shiny marble and rich wood, seemed like an overlord's lair. And in many ways, it was. Kings were just evil overlords for humans. At least goblins were honest with themselves about being subjugated. Humans had to justify their lack of freedom with ceremonies and funny religious hats.

Eric smiled down at him as they walked towards the throne. Eric looked much better now that he wasn't a rotting zombie, although Skwee didn't notice much change in the smell. Eric's face was back to its grotesque pink hue, but Skwee had been around humans long enough to know it was what they considered perfectly healthy.

Rose followed beside them, and for the first time he could remember, she wasn't wearing the metal contraption on her back. She said it needed repairs, but Skwee wondered if her injuries might be the real reason. She walked with a slight limp despite all the potions and healing balms they'd tried. Necromantic magic could be like that sometimes. There was a good chance that sacrificing a goat would heal her immediately. But no one had asked for his opinion on the matter.

They reached the throne. The King sat atop, looking down at them with a grin. 'Ah, my saviours!' he announced, great moustache wobbling with glee. 'What would I do without you! Just the three of you, is it? That uh... *Xenixala* isn't here, is she?' His eyes glanced nervously at the door.

'Just the three of us,' said Eric, his voice hoarse.

Skwee was relieved that the nasty witch had decided to abandon them hastily once they returned to the Beast Be Gone shop after defeating Edwardius. She said something about getting "the worth of words," made some curt goodbyes, and then disappeared into thin air. All that she left behind were bat droppings, which Skwee had the pleasure of cleaning up.

Larry had volunteered to stay on guard at the shop. As the mimic put it, "Furniture and outdoors don't mix. I've had enough of that for a lifetime *thankyouverymuch*." Then he'd clomped into the corner and turned into a handsome coat rack.

'Jolly good,' said The King. 'So you managed to deal with those adventuring zombies after all. It was fortuitous that I set you onto them when I did. They took over the whole city in a matter of weeks! It's a shame you couldn't have figured it out sooner. I had to barricade myself in the palace. Three perfectly good shipments of oysters went to waste!'

Eric grunted. 'We did our best.'

'Of course, of course,' The King nodded and waved a dismissive hand. 'I'm just glad the dreadful business is behind us. A necromancer called Edwardius, was it? Something about revenge?'

'Something like that,' said Eric.

'Classic necromancer, if you ask me. Such a gloomy lot. Overly sensitive, too. Probably weren't hugged enough as children.'

'I suspect not.'

Rose stepped forward. 'What happened to the people? Did everyone get their soul back?'

'Ah, yes,' said The King, stroking his whiskers. 'I believe so. Although having your soul returned to a maimed, rotted corpse couldn't have been fun for a lot of them. Most likely went straight back to the afterlife, whatever that is. Still, thousands were saved. And it's all thanks to you!'

Rose sighed. 'That's good to hear.'

'I'm not sure this city can take another utterly devastating catastrophe,' said The King, shaking his head gravely. 'We've only just finished rebuilding after the bandits ran amok. The streets of Porkhaven are awfully dead these days, if you'll excuse the pun.'

'Um, Sire?' Skwee cleared his throat and produced a scrap of paper from his pocket. 'I have... um... a plan to help with the loss of labour.'

'Is that right, Sqween?'

Skwee knew better than to correct an overlord when they got your name wrong. 'Yes, um... well, we liberated many goblins working for this necromancer. And... well, they could perhaps be put to use. As citizens.'

'Goblin citizens?' The King let out a hearty laugh. 'Now I've heard everything.'

'It makes sense, Sire,' said Eric. 'We've run the numbers. It would also prevent this sort of thing from happening again. Goblins need leadership; they'll follow anything if they're not allowed to be part of society. A new overlord will just appear and take them on. It's a vicious cycle.'

'Goblins living among us as *people*.' The King shook his head. 'I can't quite fathom it, although I trust your judgement, Eric.'

'Um...' said Skwee. 'Goblins will work for almost no pay. Practically just scraps of food. If that helps?'

The King clapped his hands together. 'It does indeed! However, let me run it by my new Fist of The King...'

The air suddenly grew cold.

'You need me, Sire?' came a sultry voice.

The King nearly leapt out of his throne. 'Lady Vanderblad, what did I say about sneaking up on me like that?' He breathed a sigh. 'You'll be the death of me.'

Lady Vanderblad's mouth twitched. 'I do hope not, *Sire*.' She had an eerie appearance. Her tight black clothes seemed to absorb all light. A crimson circlet held her white hair perfectly still. She was precisely the person you'd avoid shaking hands with at a party. Not that Skwee had been to many.

'This is Lady Vanderblad,' said The King. 'My new *Fist of the King*. My right-hand person. She's been very helpful with arranging the clear-up. The corpses disappeared overnight. Astonishing work. Not a drip of blood left on the streets.'

Lady Vanderblad bowed. 'Only the best for the realm, *Sire*.'

Skwee didn't like how she kept saying "Sire". It sounded somehow like a veiled threat.

'Vanderblad here only works in the evenings, so I don't get to see her much. But she gets things done, and that's all that matters.

Eric looked her up and down. 'I'm sure she's been *vamping* things up around here.' He smiled and winked at Vanderblad, who scowled.

'Did you hear their idea for the goblins?' asked The King, absent-mindedly scratching at his neck.

Lady Vanderblad nodded. 'I did. A most *excellent* idea, *Sire*. Goblins are malleable creatures. Even more so than humans. So long as we keep them from positions of power, they could be a useful workforce to replace the losses from this recent... incident.'

Skwee beamed. This was a fantastic leap forward for goblin equal rights. Maybe one day, he could even be king. King of a small swamp or something. Nothing too big, but definitely wearing a crown.

'Marvellous,' said The King. 'That's settled, then. Vanderblad, I'll let you figure out the details. Eric, would your company be willing to assist? I'm sure the goblins may need a little persuading. And uh... socialising.'

'Of course,' said Eric. 'For a price.'

'Naturally!' The King laughed. 'Speaking of which, I have your rewards. You can't save a kingdom without some rewards, now can you? It wouldn't be right. I would like to offer you...' He paused for effect. 'My daughter's hand in marriage.'

'Oh...' said Eric, rubbing the back of his head. 'That's very kind and all... but... wouldn't that make me... king one day?'

'Oh no, no, my dear boy. I have dozens of daughters! And most of them are already betrothed. More importantly, one of my sons will no doubt take my place. No, you can marry Helena if you wish. She's a little plain, but still, a princess is a princess.'

'But isn't she... seven?'

'Almost eight!' said The King. 'But don't worry about that. They grow up awfully fast.'

'I'll pass, thank you.'

'I thought you might say that.' The King sighed. 'As you wish.' He clapped his hands together. Servants marched into the room carrying a large wooden chest. They heaved it down in front of The King, bowed and left. The King opened the lid, casting a golden glow across their faces.

Skwee licked his lips. They could buy a lifetime supply of rat pie with all that treasure.

And even have spare left for dessert.

EPILOGUE

Level Seventy-Three Conjurer Xenixala of Xendor, Viscount of Vampires, Champion against The Plague of The New Master and bronze medalist at the Best Groomed Bat awards, flapped in through the open window. The necromancer's tower was tall yet totally unprotected from the sky. Was this Steven going to be as powerful as Eric promised? He didn't even have any protective wards set up.

She turned back into a vampire for what may be the last time, landing on the stone floor of the bedroom. She looked around and shuddered. All along the walls, zombies stood or sat in various positions, each a twisted imitation of some kind of furniture. Some stretched their arms out, holding coats like a coat rack. Others were on all fours draped in a table cloth, while some simply looked upwards, with a candle glowing out of their mouths.

Xenixala grimaced, covered her nose and went over to the figure lying in the bed.

'Wake up,' she barked.

'Good grief!' The figure yelped and leapt out of bed. 'How did you get in here?!'

Xenixala gestured to the open window. 'Steven, is it?'

The man wore a loose, purple gown, revealing a pale, lithe frame. 'Indeed,' he said sheepishly. He closed his robe and tied the silk belt. 'With a V. But please don't kill me... I've got so much left to die for.'

'I'm not here to kill you.'

'Are you here about the smell?'

'Not quite. Steven-With-a-V, I have need of your expertise.'

'Oh... I see.' His shoulders relaxed as he pointed to one of the zombies hunched on the ground. 'Please, take a seat.'

'I'll stand, thanks.'

Steven plopped onto one of the zombies, which made a faint squelch. 'Suit yourself.'

'I hear you're quite the powerful necromancer. Is that true?'

'Oh really? By whom?'

'A pest control agent called Eric.'

'Ah, yes, a lovely fellow. Tony Bones thought he was a little grumpy, but he's a skeleton, so not such a great judge of character.'

'That's him, alright. Well, are you one?'

'Am I what?'

'A powerful necromancer?'

Steven looked around at the zombies in the chamber. 'I like to think of myself as more of an *artist of the death*. None could do what I do.'

Xenixala nodded. 'Excellent.'

'So what can I do for you? I suspect I don't have much choice in the matter.'

'You don't.'

'Fair enough.'

'I need you to reunite me with my soul trapped in The Underworld.'

He sniffed the air, slowly at first, then rapidly. He sighed. 'I thought I smelled something undead about you. That could be a little tricky, though.'

Xenixala took out the scrap of Wordsworth's page and the note with the incantation. 'I received these from The Underworld's Librarian. He said they would make sense to a mighty necromancer.'

Steven put on his moon-shaped, pink-hued spectacles, took the papers and squinted at them. After a moment, he mumbled something and leaned back. 'Yes, I suppose that could work. However, it's not something I've done with the soul of a book before. Please, follow me.'

He led her down a spiral staircase and into his laboratory. Mutilated body parts hung from the ceiling, and dozens of workbenches caked in blood filled the room. Glass jars and apparatus lay scattered across the floor and shelves. Flies buzzed everywhere.

'Normally,' said Steven as he cleared the cleanest-looking worktop, 'for a human soul, you would extract a lock of hair or some-such. But this scrap of paper will have to do. It will bind back from The Underworld. Reunite body and soul.' He took out a small dagger carved from bone. Strange runes throbbed along its hilt. 'Your hand, please.'

Xenixala hesitated, then held out her hand.

Steven sliced her palm while muttering words she didn't recognise, then thrust the paper deep into the wound. He continued to chant as the candles went out. A blue light emanated from her palm.

Wind rushed into her lungs.

The force swelled inside, filling her up and up. She tried to breathe, but nothing came. The chanting grew louder and louder as the twisting mist whipped at her very core. She closed her eyes, but all she could see was light.

A light that took her. A light that exploded from within.

Then nothing.

She fell to the floor, panting. She retched, spitting blood.

She wiped her mouth and stood up. Her teeth felt oddly smooth. The world seemed brighter all of a sudden. Her skin felt warm. It felt alive.

'Are you alright?' asked Steven, pushing back his greasy black hair.

Xenixala nodded and steadied herself on the workbench.

On top of which sat a book.

'Wordsworth?!' she cried.

'Xeni!' exclaimed Wordsworth. He leapt into her arms, and she held him tightly against her chest.

A strange contentment melted through her. It was a similar feeling to when she stopped Edwardius. It was as if helping other people had its own magical properties. She'd done the right thing and saved the land, even though it almost cost her a soul. And that somehow filled her with a tingle that wouldn't go away.

'I missed you, Wordsworth,' she said with a smile.

Wordsworth riffled his pages. 'Promise you didn't read any other books while I was gone?'

She laughed. 'Of course not. But only because I was too busy looking for you.'

'Very touching...' Steven had begun to tiptoe towards the door. 'I'll, uh... be going now.'

Xenixala's eye caught something in the corner of the room—a magic mirror. Steven noticed that she had looked at it and stepped to block it from view, but it was too late.

'What's that?' she asked.

'Oh, uh... nothing,' said Steven, a bead of sweat dripping down his forehead. 'Just a little training program I've been running.'

'Training?' Xenixala strode to the magic mirror and tapped the glass.

The magic mirror sprung to life, whereupon a skull logo flashed across the reflection. *'Welcome to the evil necromancer training seminar, Part One of Seven. Thank you for choosing Steven Rotbarrow, Necromantic Services Inc. as your guide. Please remember to like, share, and subscribe. Simply ask at your local owlery...'*

'You've been training other necromancers?' asked Xenixala. She tapped on the mirror again and it went quiet.

Steven stood perfectly still. 'Well, yes... I have to make a living, you know. Haha.' His laugh had no emotion in it. 'My pretties need to be fed. You understand.'

Xenixala's eyes narrowed. 'You didn't happen to sell it to someone called *Edwardius*, did you?'

'Oh... yes... ah...' Steven continued to back towards the open door. 'Now that you mention it. I think I did. Very talented fellow. Top student... He mentioned you, actually. That's right. It's coming back to me now... small world. Haha... ha.'

Xenixala smiled, flicked her wrist, and the door slammed shut.

Steven gulped. 'I can explain...'

'Wordsworth, notice anything about Steven's robes?'

'I do indeed,' said Wordsworth. 'Robes of Everdeath. If I recall, they make the wearer *exceedingly* vulnerable to ice magic.'
'They do indeed.'
Steven scrambled to take off his dressing gown.
But it was too late.
'Ice to meet you,' Wordsworth quipped. A ray burst from his pages and struck Steven in the back.
Steven turned blue, then white, then clear. A gentle mist sparkled from his frozen form.
'Good riddance,' said Xenixala.
Wordsworth shut his pages and leapt to the floor. 'That was fun. I haven't had a good bit of adventuring in *ages.*'
'I've probably had too much, if I'm honest.'
'How about we go to an inn, get drunk and see where the night takes us?'
There was a faint groaning sound. Suddenly, all of the corpse furniture shifted. They stumbled, wailing as their souls returned to broken, twisted bodies. The poor, wretched creatures tore desperately at themselves. The ones with mouths began to scream as they looked down at their half-rotten flesh.
'Excellent idea, Wordsworth,' said Xenixala. 'But first things first. Let's kill some dead.'

THE END

Undead Don't Die

Want More Comedy?

Get A **Free** Short Story By A L Billington:

OUR UNDYING LOVE

"Jeremy was in love with Queen Ninatutu the Third. Ever since he saw her on his first day at work those twelve-and-a-half glorious years ago, he knew he was in love. Unfortunately, she didn't love him back. How could she? She was dead..."

As a thank you from Billington Publishing, we would like to offer you **free** access to **Our Undying Love,** A L Billington's short comedy horror story.

Simply go to **BillingtonPublishing.com** and sign up to the newsletter. Enjoy!

ACKNOWLEDGEMENTS

I would like to royally thank the following delightful people for all their proofreading efforts and support, as they had to endure this book at its worst!

In alphabetical order so they don't get jealous:

Dr Andrew Billington, Butch Weitzel, Cheryl Lanyon, Elena Makarenko, Eric Pankoke, Henry Billington, JB Anderson, Jeff Loftin, John Higginbottom, Laura Bienvenue, Marci Dunker, Martin Swinford, Michael Tipton, Nancy Tropkoff, Niall Gordon, Peter Thomson and Shawnie Small-Kinnear.

Billington Publishing

If you would like to get in touch, please email us at:
info@billingtonpublishing.com

ABOUT THE AUTHOR

Who is A L Billington? Some say he is just a myth, a phantom, a whisper on the lips of a kindly gentleman. Or maybe he's just some bloke with access to a word processor and too much time on his hands. Who calls them word processors these days anyway? Turns out A L Billington is old enough to use the term 'word processor', yet only ironically, which should tell you exactly how old he is. He's also the one writing this bit, so it's very strange that it's in the third person.

In case you were wondering, the 'A' stands for Arthur, and the 'L' stands for a secret that he'll never tell you unless you get him drunk at an awkward party.

Anyway, you all have access to your own word processors, so you can look him up using the magic of the internet. He's the cheeky chap who set up 'Billington Publishing' (in case you hadn't made that connection based on the narcissistic naming), therefore you can find his updates at *billingtonpublishing.com*.

Well done! You actually read this last boring bit. Does anyone actually care about the acknowledgements and this sort of nonsense? It's just a list of names, so I suppose it's a bit like watching the credits. In a way, this silly bit is like the bonus at the end of a Marvel film. What I'm trying to say is that this book ought to be as famous as Iron Man 2.

Please tell your friends it's better than Iron Man 2.

AUTHOR REQUEST

Can I ask you for a very small favour? Would you consider leaving a review on Amazon and/or Goodreads? It's very simple, you just need to log onto Amazon, click on your name at the top and go to your orders page.

If you are reading this on Kindle, at the end of this book, Amazon will display a "Before you go" section, asking you to "Rate this book". Please spare a second to simply click on the stars to rate it.

Your feedback is important to me, and will really help the book get noticed!

Many thanks!

A L Billington

ERIC AND FRIENDS WILL RETURN!

Here is a sneak peak from the next book in the series:
Beast Be Gone, Throne of Games
Coming soon to an online-retailer-near-you...

-

Skwee, the goblin, shivered as they descended into the palace cellar. The stone steps felt like ice against his bare feet. The air was thick with the scent of carrots and old rope, which Eric had said was the hallmark of a basilisk's lair. Ordinarily, this would have been a warning sign to stay away, but in this particular instance, it was the exact thing they were looking for.

They finally reached the bottom of the stairs, and the warmth of the straw-covered flooring made Skwee sigh. He looked back at his companions, Eric and Rose, who smiled and gave him the thumbs up, their faces lit by their flickering torches.

The young Rose wore her signature Western metal backpack, out of which stretched a golden claw. Ordinarily, the pack chugged and emitted a kind of steam, but Eric had told her to keep it quiet to stay sneaky. Although Skwee suspected Eric couldn't stand the sound of it.

Eric looked as he always did: messy, greying brown hair, three days of stubble and a belt that his stomach insisted on spilling over.

They all wore their matching Beast Be Gone overalls, which must have been white at one point. In the pest control business, fluids fall on you as the rain falls in the West. Or at least that was how Eric put it.

Eric stopped and knelt. 'The King was right about one thing,' he said. 'There's definitely a basilisk down here.' He brushed aside the rushes, picked up a metal disc, and examined it in the torchlight. 'One of its scales. Tough as steel, light as a feather. Smooth as silk. Such a shame it dissolves in the daylight. Could make for handy plates.'

'Or armour,' said Rose.

Skwee thought it would be better used as a hat. 'Why does a basilisk want to hide in a cellar anyhow?' he asked. 'Do they like wine?'

Eric chuckled to himself. 'Only if by wine, you mean red, oozing liquids, then yes.'

Skwee thought for a moment. 'Oh, you mean blood?'

'Right,' said Eric. 'But to answer your original question, much like ordinary snakes, they prefer the dark and damp. Cellars fit the bill perfectly. This one has taste. The palace cellars are quite a choice.'

Skwee wasn't sure if snakes preferred dark and damp. He'd seen them hiding all over evil overlord lairs. Maybe they just liked evil. Evil liked dark and damp, that was certain.

There came a clatter in the distance. Skwee carefully stepped behind Eric. 'How many people did The King say it killed again...?'

'Three palace guards and one nobleman,' said Eric, lowering his voice. 'So far.'

Skwee gulped.

'Keep an eye out for their bodies,' said Rose. 'For all we know, the alleged victims could just be missing. They could have gotten drunk in a tavern or something.'

'There won't be much left of them if it were the basilisk,' said Eric, shaking his head. 'But don't worry, we have a weasel to keep us safe.'

The cage rattled in Skwee's arms.

'Careful, Skwee,' said Eric. 'You don't want to upset the little fella.'

'I'm doing my best.' Skwee steadied the cage and made the hushing sound he'd been practising all afternoon. The cage stopped shaking.

'Hold on,' said Eric, peering through the wooden bars. 'Are you sure that's a weasel?'

'Of course!' said Skwee, puffing out his chest. 'You said that basilisks hate the odour of a weasel and that I was to go out and buy one. So I did.'

'That's all well and good, Skwee,' said Eric. 'The problem is that it's a stoat.'

The cage squeaked as if in agreement.

'But...' said Skwee, 'the man at the shop said it was a weasel.'

Eric sighed and rubbed his temples. 'Was this the animal merchant at the end of Trustworth Alley, by any chance?'

'It was!'

'Never trust a merchant on Trustworth Alley. The punny name is the giveaway.'

'Oh.'

Rose chimed in cheerfully, 'Would a basilisk be able to tell the difference?'

Eric took the crossbow from his back and loaded a quarrel. 'I guess we'll have to find out.'

'Looks more like an otter to me,' mumbled Rose as they continued deeper into the darkness.

They passed dozens of vaulted brick archways, each packed full of dusty barrels and boxes. Eric periodically sniffed the air, nodded and carried on. But still no sign of a basilisk.

Skwee didn't know if he was safer at the front, back or middle of the group. But at least he had the stoat-and-or-weasel to protect him. He'd decided not to give the furry creature a name in case he had let the basilisk have it for dinner. But secretly, he'd begun thinking of him as Wes.

Skwee took a crumb of bread he'd been saving and held it into the cage. A little brown face and button nose sniffed the air, then snatched the food from his fingers. He liked Wes, even if he was a stoat.

'Quiet,' whispered Eric as he looked round the next corner.

They stopped and pressed themselves against the wall. The cool dampness of the brick was a joy to Skwee's sweating hands.

'He's right there,' Eric continued in a hushed tone. 'Goggles on, and remember how we practised.'

They did as instructed and pulled their remodelled goggles over their eyes. The top half had been customised with an angled shade, making it impossible to see up without bending your head.

'Whatever you do,' said Eric seriously, 'don't look it in the eye.'

Skwee nodded, then realised Eric probably couldn't see him, so he gave a thumbs up for good measure. Eric had explained that if you looked a basilisk in the eyes, something very bad happened. Something about frozen stones. Whatever it was, it didn't sound very nice.

Rose and Skwee crept after Eric around the corner, keeping an eye on his shoes, which was all they could see. Presumably, the beast was up ahead.

Skwee couldn't resist a peek. He bent his neck back, and stared through the bottom half of his goggles.

He immediately regretted his decision.

The hulking serpent coiled around a gigantic barrel. Its silver scales and spines shimmered in the distance. It bared its foot-long teeth as it yawned, revealing a daggered tongue. Slime dripped from its mouth, which hissed as it left divots on the floor.

Skwee was lucky the creature hadn't seen them yet. He took a deep breath.

The basilisk was only a snake, really, Skwee told himself. Snakes weren't so bad. They were just misunderstood. As chief charmer for an old Dark Master's snake pit, Skwee had gotten quite used to them—after the initial bites and strangulations, of course. The poor things kept getting crushed under adventurers who fell into the trap. He felt terrible for them while clearing up the mess. Most snakes were actually pretty harmless. Mostly.

Eric stopped and made the hand signal.

Rose pulled three mirrors from her pack and handed one to Skwee. It had a handle on the back, which made it into a kind of shield. Skwee remembered his cue and opened the cage.

'Good luck, Wes,' he whispered as Wes leapt out with a squeak.

Wes paused for a moment and looked at them, then over to the basilisk. Wes hissed and charged straight towards the beast.

The basilisk roared.

The room thundered as the serpent swung its tail and collided with a wall. Dislodged dust cascaded from the ceiling.

'Now!' cried Eric.

Skwee's arms shook as he held up the shield.

Everything turned upside down.

Pain shot through his body as he collided with something hard and brick-like.

Rose screamed, Eric shouted, but Skwee could barely hear them over his ringing ears.

The basilisk swung at them again. Lucky for Skwee, he was already on the floor, and the tail sailed over his nose, missing it by an inch.

Skwee rolled behind a barrel, then sat up and readjusted his goggles. The mirror lay shattered on the floor. He grabbed a shard and held it high over the barrel. In the reflection, he saw Eric and Rose duck under the thrash of the serpent. Wes screeched in the distance.

The basilisk bit down on Eric's mirror shield, tearing it from his grip. Eric flailed wildly, clearly unable to see where the attack came from. Fighting an enemy you couldn't see was harder than it looked. Quite literally.

Rose's backpack claw had sprung into life. Unhindered by the burden of goggles, it struck at the basilisk's face. Steam whizzed. The claw clanked uselessly off its scales.

The great jaws bit down, ripping the contraption from Rose's back in one fluid motion. Sparks crackled and died as the basilisk shook his head and swallowed the metal whole.

Rose whimpered and scrambled away.

The basilisk rose to strike again.

Rose needed help. She couldn't even see it coming.

Skwee could only think of one thing that could help now...

And it was Wes.

To be continued...

Milton Keynes UK
Ingram Content Group UK Ltd.
UKHW032358031124
450530UK00001B/8